# Hive

Rowan Redfield

Editor: Maggie Burns

❀ Formatted with Vellum

*This one is for Maggie, who immediately got the hype about the bees, and to all you freaks who also can't wait to see what happens in the Hive.*

# Also by Rowan Redfield

**The Shadow Sequence**

*Heir of Fates*

*Vessel of Shadows*

**Other**

*The Snow Thief's Amulet*

*Become the Beast*

*Above the Oculus*

*Hum, Hum*

Oh the house of denial has thick walls
and very small windows
and whoever lives there, little by little,
will turn to stone.
In those years I did everything I could do
and I did it in the dark—
I mean, without understanding.
I ran away.
I ran away again.
Then, again, I ran away.
They were awfully little, those bees,
and maybe frightened,
yet unstoppably they flew on, somewhere,
to live their life.
Hum, hum, hum.

— Mary Oliver, an excerpt from *Hum, Hum*

# 1

"Scientists said we would have another hundred years once the last ice melted," I say as I walk across the stage. "But their predictions were wrong. We never really stood a chance. Not when the rains came or the drought that followed. Not when the wind stoked the wildfires."

A student in the front row with a name I can never remember raises her hand. "But, professor, what about the moon colony?"

"What about it?"

Her brows furrow. "Why didn't they save us?"

I resist the urge to scoff and remind myself that I was once an eager student too. Even more so, I was a desperate-to-prove-myself naive one. Now, I'm just a desperate-to-prove-myself adult masquerading as a science professor.

"The moon colony was made for the elitist class. By nature—or by design if you would like to argue it—human civilization would have destroyed itself on the moon." I tap my lecture stick against the palm of my hand before I turn away from my student.

I walk steadily back across the stage, slide clicker in hand, glancing up at the projector slides splayed on the wall. The image of the last cornfield flickers to one of a hive of bees. The corners of my mouth tug upward. It's the last apiary; one that belonged to my family centuries ago.

"During those times the science community was ignored which was a grave mistake made by the government. We warned them that humans wouldn't last much longer once all the bees were gone, but they wouldn't listen. If they had taken the early signs seriously far more people would have been saved." I swallow.

A different student from the front row raises her hand. "Professor, is it true that the crew of Project Honey went crazy and killed one another?"

I hesitate, a lump forming in my throat. It had been over a decade ago since my grandfather's mission was launched; the last effort to establish a colony of bees on a far off planet. The crew never returned.

"We will analyze the failure of Project Honey in module three." I try to relax my shoulders, but the student still stares at me. "Insanity is the speculated cause of the failure, but we cannot know for certain unless another crew is sent to Galactica."

The student frowns, cocking their head to the side. "Would The Company do that? Send another crew?"

I'm not sure, and I don't know how to tell the student that either. The Company has denied proposal after proposal for an investigation mission for years. The planet is habitable, but it doesn't seem like The Company wants to invest the time in sending another potential failure out there.

"I'm not sure, but if they see the payout is worth it, they might," I reply, with a smile.

I use the clicker to turn off the projection and raise the lights in the hall. Only twenty students sit in the room that could seat two-hundred. It takes everything in me to not let the disappointment sink in. Sooner than later The Company will start to note the dwindling interest in my studies and put me at risk of losing my tenure. Instead, I fake a smile and walk toward the podium.

"This semester you will learn all about how bees and many other insects influence the natural environment." I shuffle around the papers. "Your first reading is the—"

A lone figure is standing in the back of the room. Nice suit, hair slicked back, but a stony expression. He's so well put together. Nothing like my disheveled, larger than life, golden curls that spring from my head or the nicest white button up I own, still stained with coffee from this morning. A lump forms in the back of my throat, and my hands tremble as I place them on the wood podium.

"Dr. Jensen?" a student asks.

I shake my head. "You'll find it in your syllabus. Class dismissed."

The students shuffle out as the figure glides forward. I remain where I am, attempting to not let my body break into the shakes. He takes his time, scanning the room. I imagine he is waiting until we're alone which can only mean bad news. I pull my curls up into a knot on the top of my head, brushing the stray strands that fall in front of my face, blocking my vision.

*Is the program getting defunded? Is The Company cutting my class?*

I relax my shoulders, unclench my jaw. I would have been fired already if they knew of my past transgressions. I've barely begun teaching this semester; they can't already want to cut my class. My mind races as I fly through each possible reason for this visit, but my scattered brain can't settle on one idea. If I had just taken my afternoon meds this wouldn't be such a problem.

*You idiot, how could you forget your medications?*

The suit-and-tie man stops shy of the stage. Even from this distance he's intimidating. "Dr. Hannah Jensen?"

I'm parched. "That's me."

"Good." His lips pull into a tight line. "I've been told to come fetch you."

"May I ask why?" I raise a brow, rearranging my papers again. *I'm getting let go. Fired. Disposed of.* My stomach flips and my muscles tense. My father told me this would happen if I pursued this route of study. He told me not to waste my time chasing my grandfather's dreams, that it would only put me under further scrutiny of The Company. In fact, I believe his exact words were, 'You'll become useless to them as a teacher, and then they'll float you.'

Encouraging. So, so encouraging. It's what every daughter wants to hear—that their employer will kill them should they become expendable. The lump in my throat becomes impossible to swallow.

The official hands me a manilla envelope, his tight lined lips cranking up into an uncanny grin. "You've been funded, Dr. Jensen. Congratulations."

My heart completely stops, and I freeze in place.

*Could it really be...?*

Slowly, I open the envelope to reveal my grant submission —a mission to Galactica, the planet that took my grandfather's life. Tears sting me, and I choke up. This is what I prayed for every night, and it's what I've worked so hard for. Someone is finally giving me a chance.

"Say it again," I demand. I need to know I didn't mishear him.

He cocks his head to the side. "Project Nectar has been fully funded. Now, come on, we need to get the paperwork signed and introduce you to your crew."

# 2

An oak table fills the room. I run my hands across the rough texture. There's no resin to seal the wood, and it smells delightful. It's lavish, a luxury most couldn't afford—or, more so, a luxury The Company would never let anyone else indulge in. I'm surprised even The Company would bother with such a novelty in wake of their own research. The piece is clearly imported. Perhaps made by another organization established far enough away not to be a threat.

"I am sure you are well aware that you will be required to follow all protocol," the lawyer, Parker, says. He slides a new stack of papers to me. "There are some special requirements on a mission so long. Have you ever been in any atmosphere before?"

I shake my head at the ridiculous question. Of course I haven't; I've never been anywhere. Shouldn't it be in their file that I've only done the basic gravity and anti-gravity training?

my stomach sinks. What if they have the wrong person? Did my file get mixed up with someone else's?

"Just confirming. Your crew should be able to show you

the ropes if you are comfortable with it, or do you feel you need training before you go on this mission?"

"When do I meet them?"

He coughs twice and motions to some suit standing by the door. The suit disappears for a moment before returning with a tall, dark, and handsome man. His square face is complimented by a wide grin. He carries himself with an aura of professionalism, but the sweat beading on his brow doesn't go unnoticed.

"Dr. Jensen, meet Captain Jasper Norman. He has served almost twenty years in the military, and he's excellent," Parker says. "He will be leading the expedition alongside his crewmates, Officers Mari June and Elijah Tomms, and Chief Military Commander Arthur Connelly will also be joining you."

Captain Norman reaches a hand across the table to shake mine. I do so nervously because I *know* who he is. On their last mission, he and his crew destroyed millions of dollars worth of The Company's property due to pure negligence. It was all over the tabloids. Pairing them with my mission had to be a slight from The Company because surely I deserve better than the worst crew.

Captain Norman takes a seat across from me, next to Parker who slides another packet in the captain's direction.

"Can you go over the details again?" Captain Norman asks Parker and me.

I jump in before Parker gets the chance. It's *my* mission after all. "The expedition is to Galactica 23.We're hoping to establish a colony of bees that will support life for a human colony."

"A *super-human* colony," Parker corrects as if I care about The Company's requested modification. It isn't like I'll be the one working on it. Besides, I might be colonizing the bees for

The Company, but I have plenty of my own reasons for wanting to go to Galactica.

"Haven't we sent a crew that way before?" Captain Norman asks.

"Yes," I snap at him, "but they failed. We won't."

He flinches and frowns but doesn't add anything else. I divert my attention back to the paperwork in front of me. Everything in this proposal is solid. It's all in order. There's no reason not to sign it, and yet...

"There is something I should warn you about before we meet with the board," Parker says, averting his gaze.

"Go ahead," I say as I begin to sign.

"The board is going to ask you some pretty harsh questions," he says, his tone short. "They ask that you have an open mind about it and consider your answers carefully."

I stop signing and look at him. I grit my teeth together and count back from ten because this is all I've ever wanted in life. There's no need to panic. This is normal—the board *always* interviews post-acceptance. It's procedural. Normal. It's *fine.*

"What sort of questions?"

He doesn't have time to answer before a slew of people walk into the room. My stomach turns and my skin tingles like a dozen bugs are crawling all over me. I'm met with four additional faces to Parker and Norman's. A beautiful blonde woman in a lab coat, an elderly man near breaths from death in a suit, a younger man with beige skin and a smile that could light up a room, and...a face I'm all too familiar with.

I clasp my hands together to keep from fidgeting. My past filters back to me, over and over in waves. Before me sits my greatest guilt—the woman whose future I stole years ago.

Dr. Brooke Keller.

Her expression is smug, lips turned up and dark eyes

narrow. Oh, the *nerve* of her. A wave of nausea washes over me. She sweeps her braids over her shoulder. The white dress she wears illuminates her dark skin. Suddenly, it's too hot in the room.

"Dr. Jensen," the blonde woman greets. "I assume Parker gave you the details?"

I nod, sliding my paperwork back across the table to the lawyer. He puts it in his briefcase. Next to me Captain Norman shifts in his seat. I wonder if he's feeling the same pressure as I am sitting before the board.

"Great," she continues. "We have a few questions about your psychological state."

"My psychological state?" I ask, my voice shrill. I can't help it even though I should have guessed they were going to ask. "What do you mean? I just had my routine evaluation and was cleared for work."

"This is only routine." She chuckles. "You see, the crew had some concerns because of your grandfather."

"I am *nothing* like him," I rush to say without even hearing her out. I don't need Captain Norman to think I'm psycho like my grandfather was accused to be. I don't need the captain even *speculating* I'm like him. "I can assure you that I am stable."

Brooke holds her chin high as the woman and elderly man lean in to whisper to one another.

"Fine, let's just get the evaluation over with," I say.

I sit and go through the same questions we're asked in every evaluation, giving the same answers I always do, and she jots them down. After she's done asking, she gives the elderly man a skeptical look. I know what I need to do even though I'm unhappy doing it.

"My grandfather was clinically insane," I say through gritted teeth. Under the table I twist my thumb back. It's horrible to tear down someone you admire, but if it's what I have to do then... I have to. That's it. "His mission failure was caused by his psychosis, and additionally, my intended research goals are *much* different. The Company has my unconditional loyalty, and I would never lie in order to be sent out."

"Very well," the blonde says. She snaps her fingers, and Parker passes her a packet. She flips through the pages.

"I'm sorry," I say, laughing lightly. "I didn't catch your name."

"Dr. Anna Todd," she says, still flipping through page after page. "You may call me Anna." She stops on the very last page. "Your record says you have been in counseling for the past fifteen years and that you are currently on fluoxetine. Is that correct?"

Cotton replaces all the moisture in my mouth. "I...yes, that's right."

"A pretty high dose too," she notes.

"There's nothing wrong with being on medication," I snap and immediately my cheeks heat. The captain scoffs beside me.

She glances at me, frowning. "I never said there was."

*It was implied.*

Brooke leans forward, capturing the attention of the table. "If I may, I do not think it would provide any additional strain for myself to supervise Dr. Jensen to ensure her stability if The Company would prefer that arrangement."

"What about your current research?" Anna asks, raising a brow.

Brooke shrugs. "I don't see why I cannot continue with my research while on the mission. The ship has a large enough lab for two, and my specimens wouldn't add any additional weight that would disrupt the travel either."

Anna's attention shifts to me and then to Captain Norman. "Captain? Thoughts?"

"I..." He shifts in his seat, leaning forward and clasping his hands together on the table. "I mean, we just want to be reinstated."

"Dr. Keller's presence would not affect your contract with us," Anna says.

"Um...then I don't have an issue with it," he replies. "We'd love to have Dr. Keller."

"Great." Anna gives my records back to the lawyer. "It's settled then; Dr. Keller will supervise."

Everything goes red while an alarm sounds in my head. "There has to be someone else."

"Pardon?" Anna asks, brows shooting up to the middle of her forehead before sinking into a scowl. "Dr. Jensen, you should be grateful that Dr. Keller has so graciously volunteered. In fact, if it were not for her, your proposal would not have even been heard at all."

My beating heart stills. I can't possibly have heard her correctly. "What?"

"Dr. Keller personally pulled your application out of thousands."

Anna was serious. Brooke really had pulled my application. *Now why would she do that?*

Perhaps she wants to see me publicly fail, or maybe it's something else. She could have any number of vengeful reasons for wanting my success. I almost ruined Brooke's life, so she should hate me, but on the other hand, she's a brilliant scientist. Even if she hates me, I could use her brains. Either way, until I know what she's trying to do, it's a pretty big risk.

"Can you agree to this arrangement or do we need to find another specialist to conduct your experiment?" Anna asks.

I ball my fists so tight I'm sure they'll leave nail marks,

hating every bit of my ambition that will soon drive me to insanity. I might've signed the contract of my dreams, but it's starting to feel more like I've signed my death warrant.

"Yes." My stomach twists. It's a mistake. "Yes, I agree to it."

Anna nods, and the entire board stands. Only Brooke leans back in her chair as she says, "I'm glad you made the right choice."

I let out a half-hearted laugh. There are no real choices once you're The Company's property.

# 3

## 5 Light Years Away

The shuttle hums as we shoot out across the stars. My breath catches as we hit a pocket of space that tosses us around. Ahead, bright yellow reflects back to us—Galactica 23. The planet is surrounded by a dozen rings, each one shimmery and golden. It's mesmerizing. Beyond the rings is the planet itself, as large as a gas giant. It's the most beautiful planet I've ever seen in my whole life, and a thrill surges through me at the prospect of setting foot on it for the first time.

"Bring us in for a slow rotation," Captain Norman says. I can see why he's in charge. His voice is robotic, commanding, and he *never* seems to relax. Not even off the clock. It surprises me that he ever let his crew screw up a mission.

"Copy," June, our Chief Navigation and Communications Officer replies. A damned good one too. "Setting speed to two-thousand kilometers..." She lets out a small sigh as the shuttle settles into the rotation. "...And, locked for the next twenty-four hours."

"Does this shitass planet even rotate at twenty-four?"

Tomms asks, chuckling as he pulls out a pack of cigarettes. Contraband, but nobody says anything about it.

It's Connelly that replies.

"You can't even count that high, so what does it matter to you?"

"Asshole—"

"Don't get upset with me, sweetheart, I'm just pointing out the truth." Connelly laughs. His orange curls fall onto his pale, freckled face. "Now pass me one of those bad boys."

Tomms tosses the pack and Connelly catches it flawlessly.

"Would you two keep it down?" Norman barks back at them. I'm grateful for his interjections because they *are* rather distracting, and I need to focus on the first steps of my plan once we make contact.

"Aw, come on—"

"Tomms, don't start with me," Norman snaps at the Chief Engineer as he runs a hand absentmindedly over his nearly-bald head. He's strapped into the front left seat next to June. A layer of sweat has collected across his dark brown skin, from nerves no doubt. After all, this is his last chance to prove himself as a captain. "Are we all clear?"

June brushes one of her braids over her shoulder. "All clear, sir."

They both unbuckle, signaling it's safe to do so, and the crew wastes no time springing out of their seats.

I lean back and savor this moment before releasing my own buckle and file into the commons—the small dining area in the center of the ship—with the others.

I hadn't much time to explore prior to our take off. The Company sent us out fast after my acceptance. One minute I was signing papers and meeting the crew, and a month later we were climbing into our pods for a nice long sleep. There was hardly any time to get to know each other. Not that it would have mattered; Brooke made it clear right away that she didn't like me, and that was good enough for everyone else to steer clear since she's The Company representative here.

Norman and June were headed to the bridge, locked in an intense conversation too quiet to overhear. There was a closeness between them in the way Norman *almost* smiles at her. Brooke was probably already in the labs down the hall behind me. Connelly and Tomms peeled off down the right corridor to our bunks, no doubt looking for trouble.

I stare at the back of their heads as they go. My stomach curls slightly as Connelly glances over his shoulder at me and winks. His auburn hair glints under the fluorescent lights, and his bright blue eyes almost sparkle. A half smoked cigarette dangles from his lips. He's ragged and worn, but there's an intrigue about him. Compared to Tomms, whose blonde hair is constantly covered in grease, Connelly is almost—

"What're you staring at, Jensen?" a demure voice asks.

Brooke Keller stares at me with a knowing smile. She steps in front of me to block my view of Connelly and Tomms. "Distracted already? Are you finding all of this too overwhelming?"

"I'm not," I protest, my cheeks heating.

"All I'm saying is that it's a *long* trip," Brooke states. "Don't forget, you actually have to do your work. Besides, I can't imagine Connelly would take an interest in someone like you."

I swallow as my nerves spark, catapulting shots of energy through me. I shift on my feet, trying to avert my gaze away from Brooke. I remind myself that she wants a rise out of me. She *wants* me to mess up, but I'm not going to—unless... I'm *not* going to mess up.

"When are we going to break atmosphere?" I ask instead of giving into her taunts.

Brooke shrugs. "If it were up to me we'd just go down."

An exasperated noise comes from behind me. Norman and June come into view and join us, forcing Brooke to lean against the metal wall of the Nectar.

"Nonsense," June says. "We need to study the topography. Send down a drone and see if what we're tracking up here is consistent down there. We need to know what the atmosphere is like, if there's *real* water, and where the safest place to land is." She takes a large breath. "And we need to know what those yellow clouds are."

"Storms," Norman says, pressing his arm against June's. "Hopefully not geomagnetic."

"Don't we already know all of that?" I ask. "We have been studying Galactica for decades."

I raise a brow at Brooke and the two members in front of me. I'm just a melittologist to them and my life's work is just a chance for their redemption, but I still want my answer because I know that Galactica has water, that the clouds are storms, and that it's a perfectly safe planet.

"What's the problem?" I ask.

Norman chuckles, running a hand across his head like I've seen him do a hundred times, a nervous tick, I assume. Brooke excuses herself and walks quickly toward the lab. It's June who offers a tight-lipped smile.

"We would lose all contact with the Nectar," June says. "Geomagnetic storms affect the navigation units and communication comms during entry. It's possible we would take damage to the module."

"Oh." I should have known that. Why didn't I know that? I bite my lip, rolling back my shoulders. I need to remember things better.

"That's all you have to say?" Norman asks, sneering at me.

I open and close my mouth several times before responding. "I only thought maybe there would be—"

"Why don't you let us senior officers figure it out, and you just go check on your little bee eggs?" Norman asks, and he walks straight toward me, bumping my shoulder as he passes.

I watch him pass then turn back to June who is already walking away in the opposite direction. My stomach sinks.

"Briefing in twenty!" Norman shouts back up the hallway.

I take a deep breath, trying to distract myself from the anger bubbling within me. These people hate me, and there's nothing I can do except hope they come around. But, it's not forever. Once colonization takes hold it's back to cryo sleep and never having to see any of the crew again.

# 4

All six of us gather around the table in the commons. Tomms passes out our freeze-dried meal for the night: a bland sandwich with jerky on it and orange slices. None of us are happy about it, but we need the calories so we eat. It's a comfortable silence.

Naturally, Tomms and Connelly are the ones to break the silence with their banter. Despite not knowing one another very well, they seem to have hit it off in a way that makes green envy grow inside me. They shove one another, laughing and being obnoxious to the point that eventually June involves herself by throwing a napkin at them. Norman pointedly ignores them, and Brooke continues to quietly eat.

I keep my focus on the food in front of me. The jerky is hard, and my wisdom teeth protest in pain with every bite. *Why didn't I get these removed a decade ago?*

*Pointless thinking, Hannah.* I sigh, pushing around my orange slices. I should be thinking about how I'm going to build my brood chambers once I'm on Galactica. *But you also need to rest so you don't slip up in front of your overwatcher.*

"Dr. Jensen," Connelly says, breaking my concentration. A

large grin lights up his face. "Now that we're getting ready to land, can you tell us what we're doing here?"

I tip my head to the side. I hadn't realized they didn't know the basis of the mission. Why wouldn't The Company tell them? Before I have a chance to answer, someone else interrupts.

"Seriously?" Norman asks. He sighs, tossing his sandwich on his plate. "The bees, Connelly. That's what we're here for."

"Didn't you read your contract?" June pipes up.

"He saw the dollar signs attached to the contract and voided the rest," Tomms says.

Connelly lets out an exasperated sound. "I did no such thing."

"Really?" Tomms asks.

"Contrary to your accusation, money isn't a motivating factor for everyone," he replies.

"So you read the entire fifty page packet?"

"It was *fifty* pages?"

I bite back a laugh, at least it wasn't one hundred plus pages like mine. I imagine he didn't watch the video presentation The Company forced me to record for them either.

"What?" Connelly shrugs, picking up a slice of orange and slipping it between his teeth. Even with his mouth full, he goes on. "Don't even begin to tell me any of you read the whole thing."

"I was under the expectation that our Chief Military Commander would let us know if the mission was dangerous after reading the packet," June says. "So why would I read it?"

"Brave of you to trust someone you don't know," Connelly laughs. "I don't give a shit if the mission is dangerous. That's all the more incentive to go."

"I knew I liked you for a reason," Tomms says, grinning

and slapping Connelly on the back. "He's a good one. Can we keep him, Captain?"

Norman pinches the bridge of his nose, letting out the longest most exaggerated sigh I've ever heard. "You lot are going to drive me into an early grave. We're supposed to be the professionals here. This isn't an ordinary mission."

The captain drops his hand and stares at me intensely. "I suppose now is as good of a time as any to go over the mission brief then. Dr. Jensen?"

I fold my hands over one another in my lap, trying not to move too much as I recall the details of the mission. I should deconstruct them into layman's terms. "Right. The mission consists of two phases. Phase One is set to take ten weeks; that's when I'll be setting up the bee colonies. Phase Two—"

"Is under my direction," Brooke interrupts. She smirks at me before continuing. "Estimation is six months post Phase One that we have our first established human colony."

All four of them stare at Brooke with, from what I can tell, utter shock. My stomach boils. Even if Brooke is supervising, it's still *my* mission.

"We're colonizing Galactica with humans?" June asks.

"Hinging upon the success of being able to pollinate the planet with the bees," I add in, glaring at Brooke. "Right, Dr. Keller?" I ask, snarkily.

She shrugs. "The mission should go without a hitch."

"And after," Norman says, "we should all be reinstated without consequence with The Company."

"Right on!" Tomms shouts, fist pumping the air.

Everyone has a reason to be here. Connelly leans back in his chair, observing everyone else. Except him. He has no reason to be here. No incentive. So why *is* he here?

"Dr. Keller and Dr. Jensen are in charge of this mission," Norman says, distracting me. "Which means we *all* must be on our best behavior." He pointedly gestures at Tomms. "No tomfoolery. Got it?"

"Yes, sir," Tomms says, saluting the captain. "Won't hear a peep from me."

Norman taps his foot, impatiently.

Tomms and Connelly burst into laughter, and I find myself wishing I could chuckle with them. Once they settle down, Connelly returns his attention to me. I'm drawn to his tongue as he licks his lips.

"So, Dr. Jensen—"

"Call me Hannah, please," I correct.

"Dr. Jensen." He smirks. "Since I, obviously, don't need to read my mission packet now, why don't you tell us about you."

Tomms lets out a loud groan. "Oh, for fuck's sake... Who gives a shit?"

"Tomms," Norman warns, his tone sharp and short.

"What do you want to know?" I ask, placing my hands in front of me, lacing my fingers together. Why doesn't he want to know about Brooke?

"What type of scientist are you?" Connelly asks.

"I'm a melittologist."

"What's that?" Tomms asks.

"I study bees," I explain. Shouldn't that be obvious now? "Twenty-thousand different species. Their biology, ecology, and sociology."

"That's why you're in charge, eh?" Tomms asks.

"Technically, I'm in charge," Brooke interjects.

*Bullshit. This is my mission.* I resist the urge to grumble my complaints.

Tomms ignores her and continues, "Makes sense with the whole bee theme."

"The mission is about bees, yes," I say slowly, "but The

Company wants us to establish the hives on Galactica so the ecology can support human life. Both my own and Dr. Keller's research is important."

They all wear blank expressions besides Brooke who leans back with her arms crossed, unimpressed. Not that I expect her to be impressed by anything I say ever again. I'm an idiot, clearly, and should shut up.

"What the fuck do bees have to do with establishing another colony?" Tomms asks.

"Manners, please," Norman insists.

"Sorry," he replies, giving Norman a half-smile. "They don't have any insects on Proxima Centauri B, so why do they need bees on Galactica?"

My face flushes and I force myself to consider how to translate what I *should* say instead of what I *want* to say, which would be entirely unprofessional.

"They have to import all of their food on Proxima Centauri B," Brooke says.

I release my breath slowly, attempting to regulate myself. I don't want Brooke to answer for me. I'm smart enough without her and I can prove it too.

"Exactly," I say. "Establishing a proper ecological system on Galactica would allow humans to farm for food. Without bees to pollinate, that will be less sustainable in the long run."

Connelly leans back in his chair, placing his hands behind his head. He continues to stare at me, dragging his gaze up and down my body.

"Where did they even get the frozen bees?" Tomms asks, still making a mess of his food as he tears apart the remainder of his orange slices. "Not to be rude or anything, but I thought The Company wasn't into lab produced animals or whatever. And like, we don't have that shit on other planets."

I'm not surprised they don't know where my bees came

from; The Company has a policy that only the most important specimens are to be replicated. Unsurprisingly, they didn't find the bees useful enough to have inside our space stations. Not many people understand, but I do. It's in my blood like honey in a comb.

"Indeed," Brooke says, leaning forward and resting her chin on her hands. "It is quite an interesting tale. Why don't you share it with the others?"

*Of course she says something now.* I can't help the pang of sadness that reverberates through me. It didn't have to be this way between us, but it's my fault that it is.

Connelly props his leather boots up on the table, disturbing the rest of our food and nearly blocking my view of his face. "Enlighten us, would you?"

I'm not going to get away with a simple reply, so I need to tell the story carefully. Enough truth to satisfy Brooke, but not enough for the crew to think I'm repeating the past.

Though I am shaking as my body screams in alarm, I'm not one to back down from a challenge.

"Gladly," I say. "Sit back and relax."

Brooke's eyebrows shoot to the middle of her forehead, the smug look disappearing from her face. "Great," she says, but she can't mean it. She's curious. I need to tread lightly.

The rest of the crew settle into their chairs, their sight glued to me. Even Norman seems intrigued.

*This is my chance to get them on my side,* I think. *No, don't think like that. There are no sides in science. Just the truth.*

There is my reality and there are my grandfather's crimes. Despite his greed, I want to tell the story better than he told his own. Poetic yet harrowing. Devastating but still hopeful. However, unlike him, I want to believe the message. I don't want to negate his brilliance, but for the sake of my success I must.

"When earth ended in fire," I swallow hard, "man did everything he could, but the flames roared on anyway. The bees were doomed to die like everything else if it were not for the bravery of one man." I pause, rather dramatically, if I'm honest. "While the rest of the beekeepers fled to safety, he went back. He collected a single hive, not knowing what would become of it, but knowing the fate of our existence depended on saving those bees."

All five of them are on the edge of their seats leaning forward. Connelly's expression is masked with unwavering darkness, a melancholy that threatens to eat me alive. There's something personal in this story for him too.

"My great ancestor was that man," I say. "He saved a small section of the hive, maybe one-hundred, and froze them. He hoped that one day we could bring them all back."

My palms are sweaty, and I shuffle my feet, growing uncomfortable in my seat with the weight of the entire species on my shoulders. Is this how my grandfather felt when he was in my shoes? When he was about to land on Galactica himself? Did he think he was going to create a better future for my mother and me?

"The Company spoke of saving the bees as a species for centuries, yet we were never able to create a plan for repopulation—"

Brooke snorts, "Yeah, until your crazy grandfather came along."

I ignore her comment and continue, but my voice is thin, and my pitch creeps upward. "My grandfather made it his life's work to find a way to bring the honeybees back to life. He had a big dream, and he sought to see it come full circle."

"Your whole family studied bees?" June asks.

I shake my head. "No, not all of us had the passion."

Brooke lets out a small laugh. "You mean not all of you are insane."

"That's not—"

"Rick Carlson was a sociopath with little to no allegiance for the field of science," Brooke states. "He was barely tolerated by The Company. I am surprised they even let you pursue a science degree let alone head a mission."

I flinch, and I want to bury myself alive.

"You're Rick Carlson's granddaughter? The guy who murdered his crew?" Tomms' jaw drops. "No fucking way."

"The Company should have told us!" June shouts. She turns to Norman. "Did *you* know?"

Norman attempts to reply, but before he gets a chance to answer Tomms starts up again. "How are we supposed to believe she's not crazy too?"

Embarrassment curls within me, wanting to blossom like a weed. Sure, my grandfather might have been a bit impractical, maybe even a little too experimental, but he was *not* insane. I'm not insane.

"My grandfather was an innovative biologist who was hired by The Company to create bioweapons for the military," I say, lifting my head up. "He was brilliant."

"Sure, he only bioengineered *super-wasps,*" Tomms says, flippantly. "Going against mission security to do so, by the way."

June pushes back her chair. "This is ridiculous. They should be paying us extra for this."

Darkness embraces me, and I want nothing more than to slip away. I've lost their confidence now.

"I've read Dr. Jensen's psychological screening," Connelly says, and the table grows quiet. He stares at me as he pulls out a cigarette and sets it between his lips, without lighting it. Instead, he leans back again and places his hands behind his head. "She's completely stable. We have nothing to be worried about."

Norman nods. "Connelly's correct. I was there."

"I only thought you should know who you're traveling with," Brooke says.

Connelly glares at Brooke. "I appreciate your concern, Dr. Keller, but last I checked, I'm the security, and she's *fine.*"

"That may be the case for now, but there is a reason The Company wanted me supervising her," Brooke nearly growls out.

*You volunteered for this.* My lip curls, and disgust rolls through me.

"Whatever," June says, abruptly. "I'm out." She leaves the room.

"I, for one, hope you have a tighter head on your shoulders." Brooke brushes down her jacket. "I would hate to have to put you down."

"Great. We have a plan should things go sideways with the crazy on board. That makes me feel *so* much better," Tomms says as he snatches the cigarette out of Connelly's mouth, lighting it. "I really didn't think I'd have to worry about sleeping with a lunatic in our bunk on this mission."

"Tomms, knock it off. Connelly and I have cleared her." Norman motions to Tomms, a scowl taking hold of his face. "I thought I told you not to light those things in here. Put it out. Now."

"I'm fucking stressed, dude, let me have this."

"Tomms, I'm serious."

"You're being a killjoy," Tomms protests.

Norman slams his hand on the table. "Put it out before you blow up this whole ship."

"Not possible. The ventilation system is behind a wall of titanium."

"Would you just put it out?" Norman sighs, lowering his voice. "Please?"

Tomms curses under his breath, but he puts out the cigarette. "Whatever, man."

Norman clears his throat. "I get that everyone is upset, but arguing about it isn't going to help. We are on this mission, and we will complete this mission." He pushes back his chair. "Let's get some shut-eye. We can talk more in the morning."

Norman and Brooke excuse themselves. Tomms tosses me a lingering glance before leaving. Only Connelly and I remain.

Deep silence falls between us and neither of us move. Slowly my body calms down and I fidget less. Every moment of my life has built to this mission. Hours slaved over textbooks and journals. Countless nights spent sleepless in the labs. Dozens of grant submissions. All for a chance to correct a wrong. All to re-establish a species that will help nurture humanity. One last shot to save the bees.

"You're brave to walk in his steps," Connelly says, breaking the silence. He's not upset. Why?

"What do you mean?"

"To come out here like he did, knowing the risks."

"Oh. I suppose I'm righting a wrong." *I can't believe he's saying this.* "You must think I'm crazy."

"No. Not really." Connelly lights a cigarette and pulls a flask out from his jacket pocket, pouring the amber liquid into two glasses. He slides one across the table to me before lifting his in the air. "I don't give a damn what your grandfather did because he's not you."

I grab the glass, raising a single brow. "You aren't even curious?"

He frowns, shaking his head. "I'm much more interested in what you will do."

"I'm going to save the bees," I say too quickly.

This causes him to laugh.

"To you," he says. "Savior of the motherfucking bees."

He lifts his glass in a toast then downs the drink in one shot. My mind goes blank at the sight of the amber liquid dripping off his bottom lip.

"To the bees," I raise my glass and lean my head back, allowing the fiery liquid to burn away every last lie I've told.

# 5

The freezing tubes slide out easily; my heart floods with relief at the sight of the embryos. The Company allotted me all of the remaining bee specimens—ten-thousand eggs and one-thousand adults—enough to colonize a planet. If all goes well, the three colonies I establish will thrive in Galactica's environment and quickly grow and become self-sustainable. It'll start a chain reaction, and soon after, we will have farms that can support human life.

I pull out a thick slide of bees and run a gloved finger across one of the queens. Beauty doesn't even begin to describe her. I crane my neck down, leaning closer to get a better look at her majestic yellow and black stripes. The curve of her abdomen is divine. As I study her thorax, I imagine her antenna twitches like she is alive in my hand. Only a little while longer until that's true. A little while longer and I can finally—

I jerk back. I blink rapidly, shaking the thoughts from my head.

"You okay over there, Dr. Jensen?" Brooke asks from across the lab.

I insert the slide of bees back where they belong as I lie, "Yeah—yes. I thought one of the queens moved."

"An unnatural feat that defies explanation considering they are frozen," Brooke says, her voice tauntingly bored. She doesn't even take her focus off the vial of blue liquid she has in her hands. Only a moment passes before she says, "Have you taken your medications today?"

My jaw drops, and I clamp my mouth quickly. I remind myself that she wants to see me uneasy. "That isn't any of your business."

"I am here supervising you, aren't I?"

I scowl and say, "Yes, Brooke, I took my meds."

"Good," she says, sighing softly. "I would hate to see you grow paranoid again."

"Excuse me?"

"Like before," she continues, "During our thesis, when you used to see all of those—"

"I didn't see anything!" I snap, cutting her off. My hands shake as I turn back to the table, trying to balance myself against the cool metal. I can't let her get to me. Not now. "I am just tired, that's all. I'm perfectly stable."

The sound shuffling footsteps echoes across the room. I take several deep breaths, tempted to pull one of my anxiety meds from the plastic bag in my pocket. It's too bad I ran out of the stronger stuff.

"You know, I never liked bees," Brooke says.

The comment bothers me. Our entire dissertation was on insect pollination. Years of our lives were spent dedicated to the study of pollinators. How could she not like bees? I bite my lip. She has to be baiting me. I would be stupid to reply, but curiosity wins out.

"Why? They're harmless," I ask, daring to entertain her.

"Harmless?" she scoffs. "They sting without provocation which makes them entirely antagonistic."

*Why am I not surprised she holds such a stereotypical view?*

There's something about her tone that makes me want to pry for more. Perhaps it's her way of saying she thinks *I'm* antagonistic. It would be like her to make me out to be the villain in her delusional small world. I'm better than this. I'm better than *her.*

"Sounds like you haven't met the right bees," I reply, wanting to be done with the conversation and get back to the important work at hand, but I can't let it go. "Why did you select my grant?"

"Because your research informs my own," Brooke says. "You specialize in insects, and I specialize in humans." She raises a single brow at me. "Did you really think you'd be solely responsible for bringing human life to Galactica?

*Yes, I* will *be the one responsible for that feat.* But I don't say that. Instead, I swallow and let my blush take over my face. Brooke's always been so confident.

I pull my mug of coffee closer to distract myself. Warmth seeps through the ceramic and into my hands, and I take a long drink. It's not as good as the stuff back home, but it's easier to choke down than the sugary crap the rest of the crew drinks. Even though it does nothing for my nerves, I can't stop drinking it; something needs to keep me awake.

Brooke moves to another station and sticks the needle of a syringe into the vial she's been holding and draws back the plunger, filling the barrel with blue liquid. She picks up one of her slides containing a human embryo and injects it with the fluid.

I watch her curiously. No matter how I feel about her, I'm still a scientist.

"I developed a serum that increases the strength of

embryos in order to expedite their growth." Brooke says, answering my unasked question, and sets down her slide. Her expression lights up. "Galactica is yours to colonize with your..." Her lip curls. *"Insects."*

I clench my jaw and curl my hands under the table.

"Once I colonize the first batch of humans, I will have proven that I can not only replicate DNA at a faster rate, but I can also strengthen the genetic code to make humans nearly indestructible as a species." She picks up the frozen embryo panel. "My Galacticans will be almost immortal."

"Or they will die faster." Cruelty slips from my tongue, sweet like honey. Here we are, the two scientists going neck and neck to see whose experiment bears the most successful fruit.

Brooke's hand shakes slightly and her composure cracks for a quick second. Clearly, she did not expect me to challenge her smug attitude. And why would she? She thinks of me only as the feeble little girl, but I'm so much more than that now.

I gesture to her slide. "Did you calculate the factor of their speed of growth into how fast they will expire? You are speeding up their cell reproduction. Eventually those cells will die."

"Of course I thought of the rate of cell reproduction. I am not an imbecile," she snarls back at me.

I can tell she hadn't. She's too defensive.

I always viewed Brooke and I as predator and prey, but not anymore. I am no drone. I'm a killer bee, and I've set my sights on her.

*Stop. Consider your thoughts, Hannah.*

I lean back, letting out a slow breath as I count to ten. Like an echo in a cave I can almost hear my own words coming back to me, chastising me for wanting to tear down another scientist. The Company trusts few of us; we need to nurture one another if we're to survive. I can't be like my grandfather was with his colleagues. I must be better than that.

The spiral grows in my mind and a faint buzzing overwhelms my senses. I wet my dry lips, stumbling backward slightly. I need to be more mindful. I need to be more steady.

"I'm sorry," I say. "I didn't mean to…insult. I only wanted to point out a consideration that might help." I bite my tongue. I don't want to, but I need to compliment her—to stroke her ego. "Your work is important. I don't want it to fail."

I force a smile to my face even as the hum in my mind roars louder.

*I need to take my meds.*

# 6

"The storm lasts only four hours at a time," June explains as we gather around her. "But we might be able to slip through during this break here." She points at the footage that shows a small reprieve. "We'd have about an hour."

"No loss of comms?" Norman asks, leaning over the console toward the other screen in front of June. It displays a static graph that spikes in peaks and valleys.

June shakes her head. "No, we should be able to stay connected to the Nectar."

"Flight time?"

"Forty minutes."

Norman straightens his back before addressing the rest of us. "Tomms, Connelly, Jensen, Keller. You four will go down in the module. Find a safe place to land and scout the area to make sure it's clear."

"I would prefer that I remain on the Nectar, actually," Brooke says. "I need to guarantee the integrity of my experiments."

"What?" Norma asks.

"You see, they could be compromised by—"

"Fine," Norman cuts her off, his tone blunt. "June, you go with them instead. Keller will hang back with me."

The tension from my body releases, I can breathe again. Having Brooke off my back will be a nice change of pace, even if it's for a brief moment.

"Connelly," Norman says, "will you carry the medpack?"

"Your wish is my command," Connelly replies with a wink.

"Do *not* do that with me," Norman snaps. "You're learning too much insubordination from Tomms."

Tomms laughs. "See, he hates your antics even when you aren't being a smartass."

"Hold that tongue," Norman barks. "I'm tired of all the cursing on this ship. We have professionals on board now; learn some manners. That goes for you too, Connelly."

"Yes, sir," Connelly says.

Tomms grins. "Sure fucking will, sir."

"Hold that shit down, Tomms," Norman snaps back. He paces further into the ship. As he rounds the corner he yells, "Everyone be ready in thirty!"

Thirty minutes later the four of us—June, Tomms, Connelly, and I—are catapulted from the Nectar. My teeth slam into each other as we shoot out, faster than I've ever flown before. June pushes the throttle, pressing us into the endless night as we descend toward Galactica. Tomms lets out a holler of joy and eases back on his own handles then reaches out and turns the topography screen toward himself.

"It's gonna be a bumpy one. Hold on to your asses!" He lets out a loud laugh.

I dare a glance at Connelly. He's passed out. Snoring. I have no idea how he fell asleep so quickly.

"Unbelievable," I mutter.

"Hitting the atmosphere in three," June starts, "Two... one..."

The module jerks hard to the left. Both June and Tomms start cursing. I shut my eyes and try to keep down the bile that threatens to spill out of me. The air is rough for a few minutes, throwing our module from left to right and back again. My heart races, and my ears pop as we enter into the planet's first layer of atmosphere. The shuttle slows dramatically, forcing me to take a look.

Lightning reaches out across the sky, crackling thunder following close behind. Even inside the safety of the module, my hair stands on edge. Static warps through the glass and stretches toward us, stinging me. I blink hard several times. I reach into my pocket for one of my meds; it sticks to my throat as I swallow it.

"What the fuck is that?" Tomms asks.

I squint as I peer through the window. I can't see what he's talking about; he must have caught something on the screens.

"No, really, what is that?" he asks.

June glances at him. "I don't know, but we're approaching it fast. Heads up, everyone."

I reach over and shake Connelly as we break through the clouds. He bats my hand away, groans and turns in his chair away from me. Whatever, if he wants to miss our entry that's his prerogative. With a grunt, I shift in my seat so I can get a full view of the front window. I can't help the gasp that leaves me.

A large structure appears before us—it must be at least ten stories tall— rising into the sky, towering over the forest across the lake from it. It's building-like, but there are holes where windows should be. A golden pool of water in front of the structure shines bright in the yellow sun's rays. Everything glows in hues of saffron. As we circle closer, I catch sight of the structure. It's not like a building at all—it's a beehive.

"Bringing us around now," June says.

"Can you land us on the water's edge?" I ask.

June hesitates, exchanging a look with Tomms.

"Eh, why the fuck not?" Tomms asks. "Might as well check out the scary shit while we're here, right? It's not like anything could go wrong. Land us."

"Copy," June says as we descend further.

I can't stop observing the structure. I don't even know what to call it other than a hive. It's beautiful, but it's wrong.

The communication panel crackles and Norman's voice floods the small space.

*"Nectar to Module One, come in."*

Tomms presses the com button. "We're copying. Over."

*"Well, what do you see?"*

My ears burn, and my stomach flips. I'm glad I'm not the one at the button because I have no idea what to tell Norman. Galactica is exactly how it was described in reports, but there's something strange and eerie about the place. Tomms has a humored grin on his face as he pushes the com again.

"I think we found the perfect nest for Jensen's bees."

*"What? What do you mean?"*

June lands us, and I nearly jump out of my seat to press the comm before Tomms.

"Captain, we are reading an unusually large structure," I say, barely breathing as I keep staring through the window. "It appears to be a very large beehive, sir."

Nothing. The comm remains silent, then…

*"Jensen, I'm going to need you to be perfectly clear with me right fucking now. Are you saying there's life on Galactica?"* Norman sounds terrified.

*I* am terrified. "I don't know. There shouldn't be. The last..." I trail off, glancing at June and Tomms who hang onto my every word. "Well, sir, the reports we have say it's a barren planet, but... something created this structure."

*"Well you better find out. Connelly, you tracking?"*

I step back, turning to where Connelly sits, now awake, in his chair. His hair is messed up, and he cocks his gun, never pulling his gaze away from me as his lips pull tight before turning up.

"Oh, I'm tracking," he says. "Dr. Jensen knows how to keep a mission lively."

*"Proceed with caution. Don't mess around."*

"What he means is don't fuck up," Tomms finishes.

June visibly pales, but Tomms lets out an audible 'whoop.' Connelly appears downright crazed. I press a hand to my stomach and turn my attention back to the golden light of Galactica. It's calling me home.

I blink my tears away as anxiety swirls inside me. Black dots drift into my vision and linger.

"Dr. Jensen, I do believe this is your mission to direct now that we're on the ground," Connelly says. "What's your first order?"

June and Tomms turn, waiting for my word. I jut out my chin and stand a little taller, trying to seem like I know what I'm doing. My chest tightens, and I shove my hands in my pockets. I *can't* show weakness.

Despite the black dots still obstructing my vision and loud ringing in my ears, I turn to Connelly. "Remain close, and watch your back. We're heading out."

# 7

There's a buzz that hums to life within me as I set foot onto Galactica's surface. Golden water laps at the toes of my boots. Soft sunlight illuminates the lake, but the hive casts a dark shadow in the middle, blocking out the most intense rays of the planet's sun. A constant thrumming noise reminds me of a swarm of bees—of impending doom.

From a distance I can tell that something is wrong with the large hive. There is a dullness to its color and the caverns are wilted. *Is it even a hive?* I scan over the structure again. It's solid, clearly made as a home for some creature. There are dozens of hexagonal window caverns that presumptuously lead into the center. It certainly *looks* like a hive.

My shoes get soaked through in the warm water lapping at the shore. The pull of the waves are barely perceptible as I wade deeper. The air is thick and humid like summer. I wonder how long it will last. Galactica's seasons are tumultuous and can last as long as years or as short as weeks according to the data The Company has collected. It takes a strong species to survive such changing conditions.

"Jensen," Connelly calls behind me. His voice sounds so distant.

Thunder roars in my chest as I go farther in. All I hear is a dark, deep buzzing. I lift my hand, using my thumb and index finger to measure the height of the Hive. Did my grandfather colonize his bees in it? Was he as entranced as I am right now?

"Jensen!"

"What?" I croak out.

"Get your ass back here, now!" Connelly yells. "You're too far out. I can't protect you out there."

*Sure you can. Just use a bigger gun.* But that's not why he wants me back. He doesn't want me going off by myself because they don't trust me. How can they know how I will act? How can they trust I'm *not* just like my grandfather?

*Paranoid thinking. You haven't given them reason to suspect you, and you are not him. Not yet, anyway.*

An arm wraps around my waist and I am hoisted up, his shoulder digging into my stomach. I crane my neck back so I can watch the Hive as I'm dragged back to shore. My mind swarms with thoughts and questions. Who made the Hive? Why is it so large? What happened to my grandfather's bees? What *really* happened to his crew?

*Who or what made the hive?*

"You're a pain in my ass," Connelly mutters beneath his breath.

I want to hit him or force him to put me down but I don't. He's stronger than met. Once we're on shore, he sets me down and I take a good look at myself. My green suit is stained with golden dust. I brush a finger along it. Pollen. I shift my observation to the water beyond. A lake of pollen, falling from the Hive, I assume. My hands shake.

"What the *fuck* do you think you're doing?" Connelly

asks, raising his voice even though he doesn't have to. His hands still lingering on my waist, searing into me. His brows shoot to the middle of his forehead. He throws out his arms, waving them. I wish he'd put them back on my waist.

"Jensen. Answer. Now."

"I-I don't know," I say, my voice trembling. "I don't know what's come over me, but check this out!"

I pull my pants away from my leg, showing him the pollen fibers.

Connelly rubs his chin. "Uh, what am I supposed to be noticing here?"

"Pollen, Connelly." I reach out, grab him by the shoulders, and turn him toward the lake. "The lake is entirely made of pollen. It felt like water, but it's not."

He removes himself from my grasp and braces a hand on each of my cheeks. His breath is warm against my face and he strokes his thumb along my jawline. A shiver breaks out across my back. *Why is he touching me like this?*

"I need you to take several deep breaths," he says, nodding his head slowly. "Okay?"

"I'm breathing just fine," I snap. I attempt to tug away from him, but his grip is firm. He pulls me closer until our chests are touching.

His jaw clenches. "Jensen—"

"Oh my god. You don't believe me."

"It's not that, I just—"

"Aren't I supposed to be in charge, anyway?" I ask, raising a brow. Unsure where I got the nerve.

His face turns red. "Not when you put yourself in danger."

"Fuck off." I shove his chest, pushing him firmly away. I'm not having a breathing problem, and quite frankly, it's insulting that he assumed I'm hallucinating.

*Great, now Brooke is sharing my medical history.*

I turn on my heel and stalk off down the shoreline, brushing past a shocked June and Tomms. The crew can think whatever they want of me, I don't give a shit anymore. The lake *is* pollen, and the Hive is dead. Whatever miracle of life happened here, we're too late to see it. The heat rising from my toes to my head leaves me dizzy, but I keep walking. Sand shifts in a steady rhythm behind me. Someone is following me, and if I had to bet money on it I would say it is Connelly.

Black spots creep over my vision, and my breath grows thin. I come to a halt, placing a hand over my chest. No. Wait.

The air *is* getting thinner.

It shouldn't be. The concentration of oxygen on Galactica is lesser than it is on the ship, but I shouldn't be struggling to breathe. It's not normal. Not for here. Not for me.

I fall to my knees and in a second I'm in Connelly's arms. He's holding me against his chest, placing a small mask over half my face. I suck in pure oxygen and let out a long cough as I try to settle into the routine of breathing."

"You beautiful idiot," Connelly whispers against my head so softly I almost didn't hear. "Why don't you listen?"

I grab his thigh, squeezing tight enough to make him grunt. It's a rough sound that sends my heart cantering away. He's holding me tight, and I've never felt more secure. With his free hand, he strokes my hair, running it over my locks, down the side of my neck, along my arm. It's tantalizing, erotic, and I want him to—

"Fuck, Jensen..." He sighs, interrupting my thoughts. "What am I going to do with you?"

My vision darkens. *I have no fucking clue.*

# 8

June makes the decision that we will spend the night on Galactica by ourselves before the Nectar lands, despite it not being her decision to make. Granted, I was out cold and Norman needed an answer. I don't necessarily mind that she made the decision for me. In a way, it alleviates the pressure of it. I only hope that Brooke doesn't read it as weakness. She doesn't need any more ammunition than she already has.

Much to everyone's dismay except my own, we set our camp up along the pollen lake's edge. It doesn't take long to get settled. We all have our own small tents,so we can spend our nights in solitude, a notion that appeals to me. I need time to think about the Hive, the pollen lake, the bees. But that will be difficult since Connelly set his up beside mine because he's *concerned* about me.

I try not to make eye contact with him, but it's hard. Everywhere I turn, he's there. Staring at me. *Watching me.* As if one second I'll grow an antenna out of the side of my skull. He's being ridiculous, and he knows it. I'm perfectly fine. I don't need another babysitter. It's bad enough with Brooke hovering.

Night descends on us. Tomms attempts to make light-hearted jokes as he cooks our meal, but even June can't find it in herself to laugh. There is a stillness in the air. No crickets or lightning bugs. The waves of pollen stopped as soon as the sun disappeared. Everything is calm—waiting. For what? I don't know and I don't really want to either.

Even with the crackle of the fire, we're all on edge. Connelly studies the pollen lake as if some monster will rise from it. I blush as he catches me watching him. He raises a single brow, an all-knowing smirk coming to life on his lips. He gets some grim satisfaction from our interactions but I have no idea why.

"Dr. Jensen?" Tomms calls me to attention. "I was wondering if you had any fun theories on why the lake is made of pollen?"

"Um..." I wring my hands together, glancing over my shoulder at the large hive in the distance. I have *many* theories. None of them good. "It isn't unheard of for pollen to settle over water like algae."

"The *whole lake* is pollen though," June points out.

"Right." I can't explain it. Why do they think I can? I might be the expert on bees on this mission, but I know nothing about natural phenomena beyond that. I know nothing of magnetic fields and laws of attraction and *real* science—

*Stop it. You have earned your place in The Company. You know this stuff. You've studied.* I force myself to take a deep breath. My anxiety levels are spiking, and my lungs are shrinking. I lock eyes with Connelly. He cocks his head to the side like he's noticing the way I'm reacting. I need my meds. Now.

Lazily, as if he's trying to remain calm too, he pulls his

cigarette from his mouth. He tilts his head to the side, and his chin dips down like he's saying 'you've got this.'

*Wait, how do I know that?*

I'm actually going insane. I reach inside my jacket for my pills, but as soon as my fingers brush the lid, Connelly clears his throat. I hesitate, my breaths slowing as I descend into the depths of his view. My heartbeat slows.

"Exine-bonding," I say. Because I *do* know the answer. "The pollen could be replicating a more intense chemical bond. Mimicking the hydrogen bond in water."

June's brows crease. "I am not a scientist like you, but I'm not sure even basic chemistry works like that."

My shoulders slump, and a trapped breath escapes me.

"Why not?" Connelly asks.

"She might have a point," I admit. "Pollen can't change the way it bonds."

"You have a point too, though," Connelly replies. "We're on an entirely new planet. Proxima Centauri B wasn't what we expected either. The tides pulled in strange patterns, so why can't Galactica be the same?"

Something uneasy curls inside me at his casual mention of a discovery that shook the scientific community. He shouldn't compare Galactica to Proxima Centauri B like that. The tidal patterns on Proxima Centauri B aren't a secret, but why would a military officer like him pay attention? More importantly, why is he defending me? What stakes does he have in this?

"Wouldn't the magnetic stuff have to be like..." Tomms shrugs. "Weird as fuck?"

"You haven't a clue about anything, do you?" Connelly asks.

"Well, no," Tomms replies, shaking his head. "It's my job to know about engines and shit."

Connelly leans forward, mimicking Tomms' position. "In other words, he doesn't know shit about shit."

Tomms throws his hands up. "Okay, hold on, hold on! I know basic concepts about magnetic fields!"

"You might understand it this way then," I say. "On Earth, the magnetic field had very little to do with the way chemical bonds form, but if a planet has a *stronger* magnetic field then it could potentially influence the way atoms interact with each other. Meaning the pollen could have a different atomic makeup here."

June presses her lips firmly together.

"Especially if there are free radicals on this planet," I add.

Tomms and Connelly exchange a long look, and Connelly passes his cig to Tomms who takes a long drag.

"Radical, dude," Tomms says sarcastically.

*I'm a joke to them.*

Silence befalls us for a moment before both men fall into loud laughter. June pauses for a split second but joins in with them. I'm the only one who doesn't. It's a harsh reminder that they're not *my* crew. I'm their passenger. I wish I could seamlessly fit in the way Connelly does.

I leave them to it, trailing off to the edge of our camp, right outside the firelight. The warmth of Galactica and her sweet scent embraces me. Citrus invades my senses, but I see no fruit trees—not that Galactica should have any. I don't move as I watch the unmoving pollen. It's odd that the waves stopped splashing against the sand. Almost as if the planet itself slept at night. The Hive demands my attention. Like the lone structure, I am by myself, alien and alone. Haunted. Decayed. Unusual. Invasive.

I brush my hand over my collarbone.

*Is that really how I view myself?*

It is. I'm an invader, a species of human that lurks and

leeches from those around me. I am not to be trusted. How can I be? I barely trust myself.

Footsteps shift toward me, suddenly *he's* standing right next to me. I recognize him by his scent alone. Smoke, evergreen, and musk. It's addictive like a flower's nectar, and I'm the insect he attracts. I only wish it didn't make my body needy with want. I pray the wetness between my thighs is a figment of my imagination, but the shiver snaking down my spine at the sound of his soft sigh indicates I'm pure liquid around him.

I hate that. I've always been a desperate needless thing.

"Why does Dr. Keller hate you?" he asks. To my surprise, he doesn't light a cigarette. I wish he would. It would give me more time to think about my response between his drags. It would distract him from digging under my skin.

A blush creeps over my face, and I'm grateful for the darkness of the night that masks it. "She..." I ball my hand into a fist. "We have a complicated past, her and I. It's....I don't know, we've never really gotten along."

He huffs and jerks his head back at the camp. "They don't seem to like you either." He moves closer. The heat of his body radiates against my skin. "Why is that?"

My chest tightens as my breaths quicken.

"They don't know me," I whisper, "and the mission is strange to them. They don't understand the importance of my work with the bees."

"It's a mission. They don't need to understand it in order to complete their jobs."

"Sometimes it's easier to work toward a goal you understand."

"Sure."

"You don't think so?" I turn to face him, and my stomach flips.

He stares off at the Hive. "No, I don't." He glances at me, smirking. "I find that the more information people have, the more they tend to disobey direct orders. They get too curious. Too capable, even."

My heartbeat pounds in my ears like a hammer.

"I like my subordinates ignorant," he says.

"That's dangerous." I can hardly breathe. Does he think I'm ignorant?

"That's survival."

I swallow. Maybe I should show him my soft side here while he's inquiring. It could help him see *me* and my side. "I want them to understand."

"Do you?" He cocks his head to the side, raising a brow.

"Desperately."

He runs a hand through his hair. "I wouldn't."

"Why?"

Connelly turns fully toward me and rests a hand on my shoulder. He absentmindedly strokes his thumb over my skin, I swear I've never experienced a better feeling. His hand on shoulder. Our breaths mingling. I should step away but I don't. I want to step closer. I want him to swallow me whole.

"Jensen, you don't want these people to know you," he says. "They'll tear everything you've believed apart until there is nothing left. They're here for a paycheck. That's it."

"What makes you say that?" I ask.

His expression darkens, and his hand drops from my shoulder. "My last crew was like them. Close knit but self-absorbed. They only cared about when our next paycheck hit, not where it came from." He pulls out his pack of cigarettes, shuffling it between his hands. "People compromise their morals to be rich and famous all the time. I wouldn't want you to get caught up in that."

"Are you…" I shake my head, laughing slightly. "You don't like The Company?"

He stills, and it's the only time I've ever seen Connelly hesitate. But in a snap, he's back with that all-too-easy smile. "Listen, I'm the guy who makes sure shit gets done. Nothing more. I don't get a say in what shit-ass decisions The Company makes, and I don't want that responsibility."

"That's not really what you think," I challenge. I'm not sure why I do, but for the first time in a long time, I see a comrade in someone—in him. The Company *is* a means to an end, and I want to know what he really thinks. I want to know that I'm not alone.

He smirks. "What does it matter? We're powerless under them anyway."

"It does matter," I protest. I close the distance between us. "It matters to me."

"You…" His eyes search mine, I think he's going to lean in closer. Instead, he chuckles, breaking his gaze as he takes a step back. "The Company gets what they want, and trust me, this crew is loyal to them to a fault. Neither of us can do anything about that."

A deep itch crawls up my back like I am covered in bugs. I don't like his suspicions. I equally don't want to agree with them either, but I do.

"You really think we're so helpless out here?"

His brows furrow. "I didn't say that. I'm only telling you to be careful, Jensen."

Something in me wants to shove his advice back in his face. He doesn't know me. He doesn't know what I've been through—that I can take care of myself.

"What if I don't want to be careful? Are you going to stop me?"

He laughs, taking another step back. Now there's too

much space between us. My body ignites in rage at the distance.

"I wouldn't dream of it," he says. "If you're anything like what I've read, then I would be a damn fool to even try. You're unstoppable. A force of nature. The bee's last hope."

Everything freezes, and suddenly, nothing else matters except Connelly.

"You read about me?"

I swear his face brightens as he says, "Every last word I could find."

# 9

Galactica's sun crests the top of the Hive; the soft golden light turns the pollen lake into a rippling shimmer reverberating toward me. I am utterly entranced as the planet comes to life around me, telling me I will find all my answers here. I kneel on the soft ground and brush my palms against the gritty sand. Hints of orange and lavender are carried with the calming breeze caressing my face. Across the pollen lake, a trick of the light makes fields of tall flowers appear dark blue. Lush and beautiful, perfect for my bees.

I can already hear them buzzing as they race toward the flowers, ready to pollinate. Ready to create sweet honey for their queen.

"Jensen."

My name is barked. I'm in trouble. I remain in place, waiting for Connelly as he marches up beside me carrying a spare oxygen mask and tank. The softness I saw from him last night is gone. He's in work mode.

"What are you doing?" he asks.

"I want to go to the Hive." I lift my hand and wince from

the sunlight to observe a large crack going up the center of it. Worry gnaws at me.

"What?"

"You heard me perfectly well.".

He grunts. "Yeah, I fucking heard your delusional request." He moves into my line of vision, attaching the oxygen tank to my black vest. "We shouldn't need it, but if you start to get light headed take a few puffs."

I don't care about the oxygen. The air is fine enough as long as I don't panic. And I won't because I took a double dose of my meds this morning. Besides, what really matters is getting inside that hive.

"I need to understand it," I say, ignoring his order. "I want to know if there are any other indications of what made it, who they are, and where they've gone."

"Not happening. We're sticking to the plan *you* made, and that plan says we're doing field surveys up the hill today, so that's what you'll be doing." He loads his gun. "Let's go."

Panic hits my stomach like a brick.

"What about the Nectar? We need to land it." My voice comes out small and shrill.

Deep frown lines overtake his expression.

"We do," he says. With a grumble he admits, "But we might need another landing site."

Flutters of nerves fill my stomach. *I want to be close to the Hive.*

I grit my teeth, clamping down on my tongue. Connelly's expression softens.

"I'll let Captain Norman know that a spot near the Hive is as good of a place as any," he says, reaching out and patting my shoulder. "Alright?"

My face flushes. "Sorry, did I say that out loud?"

"Yep." He nudges me with his elbow. "Come on. Let's go."

Relief floods me as I follow after him. All that matters is the Hive. I glance at it over my shoulder, waving it a small goodbye for now. *I'll be back for you.*

June and I kneel in the grass, bagging new specimens to take back to the Nectar. Surprisingly, she's good at categorizing plants. Even though I'm the lead, and the closest scientist we have to a botanist, I let June manage herself. She doesn't need an overwatcher, and I'm hoping by letting her be, she'll trust that I have her best interest in mind.

By the time the sun is high in the sky, I'm convinced this task is too tedious. Annoyance grips me that *this* is what I have to do first instead of designing the boxes for my bees. I need a good understanding of the ecology of the planet, more so than the data we already had back at The Company, in order to find the most ideal placement. But... the Hive could be the *most* ideal placement. If only I was allowed to test it.

I sigh and bag another dark orange flower. Perhaps this one will be home to a little pollinator. I really should pay more attention to—-wait. I squint at the petals, a sudden realization hitting me. How *are* there flowers on Galactica with no pollinators?

*Oh, come on, Hannah. Self-pollination. Wind pollination. Water pollination!*

I slump. Right. I zip the bag and shove it in the crate we've brought along.

A warm wind picks up, tousling my hair. I pull it into a bun on the top of my head. I strip off my vest and jacket as the day gets hotter, tossing them next to the crate. I wonder if Connelly will lecture me about not reattaching the spare oxygen to my utility belt. I'll be fine. We're safe out here, and my medication has slowed my heart rate drastically. Not worked up at all. Not yet.

Connelly's patrol captures my attention, I absentmindedly touch the small pistol strapped to my thigh. It was a ridiculous order from The Company. We were sent to a planet void of sentient life, yet they insisted we arm ourselves with pistols and rifles and don bulletproof vests as if we never learned to handle threats during our mandatory military service.

I glance at my supplies tossed to the side. Maybe... I touch my palm to my chest, taking a deep breath. No, I'm *safe* out here. I'm only ten feet away from June and her crate. Tomms is leaning against a tree next to me. Connelly is the farthest one out.

The sun hits his short red hair just right, lighting him up like a flame, drawing me in. A cigarette hangs lazily from his lips, and his focus is on something in the distance—the pollen lake maybe or, *the Hive*. But there's something strange about the casual way he holds his rifle. It reminds me of the way my grandfather was a little too comfortable with a weapon despite never having had any formal training in the military. But, Connelly *is* hired military. At least, that's what the contract said if I remember correctly. I stand and move toward Tomms and wait until Connelly turns his back.

"Tomms, do you know what Connelly's background is?" I whisper.

"Nope. I don't know nothing," he replies, bluntly.

I drag my gaze from Connelly to fix it on Tomms. "What do you mean? You two have been all over each other this whole time. You have to know something."

"Connelly's never been with us before," Tomms replies, still working on digging up the root of a flower. "I'm still getting to know him."

*Something's off.* Connelly's comments of being the get-it-done guy come back to me like a floodgate breaking. What *is* he doing here? What if he's watching me like Brooke? My muscles quiver.

"He's just some random hire from within The Company, I think," Tomms says, sitting back with a loud sigh. "Look, he's a good bloke, and I've liked getting to know him. I hope he sticks around."

He must see the panic on my face because he rests a hand on my shoulder, squeezing once. "Relax."

"I *am* relaxed."

"No, you're fucking not." His face twists in confusion. "What's the matter with you?"

"Nothing." I shake my head, wrenching my arm away and backing up. "I'm good. All good. So good, actually."

*Don't freak out. Connelly is a random hire, like Tomms said. That's it.*

Tomms opens his mouth to say something else but closes it. He shakes his head once and without another comment, walks off to join Connelly.

My mind reels in split directions, and a headache forms at the crown of my head.

*He's not here like Brooke. He's not.*

In order to calm down, I move closer to June before continuing to work. I busy myself with plucking and bagging leaves from the tree before me. It resembles a birchwood but it's not quite right. Several feet away, the men are talking about the Hive in hushed tones like they think they're being sneaky.

Tomms leans into Connelly, that all too obnoxious smirk on his face. "You can't take her out there."

Connelly's attention drifts toward the far tree line.

"You heard what Dr. Keller said," Tomms continues. "We

have to watch her for symptoms. Don't you think taking her out to the scary ass hive is gonna trigger her?"

"Come on." Connelly chuckles. "She's not crazy."

"Are you sure about that? Because Dr. Keller—"

Connelly's face turns bright red. "I heard what Dr. Keller said, and I don't agree. Now can you lay off? My decision is final."

Tomms drags a hand through his hair, and flashes Connelly a smile, his voice growing affectionate. "Oh, I see. You have a little crush on our resident beelitologist."

"It's melittologist, and no, I don't." His tone shifts, and he turns in my direction. I duck my head, pretending like I wasn't caught staring. "But if I take her out to the Hive I can prove that it's nothing special. That's it. That's the whole point of it."

"Whatever you say, *sir*," Tomms bites out, "but I still think it's a really fucking bad idea."

"I thought you were coming around to her," Connelly says.

"Jensen's not so bad, but you heard what Dr. Keller said," Tomms replies. "She was imagining frozen bees were moving. If that's not crazy, I don't know what is."

"Give it a rest, Tomms."

Tomms storms off toward the far edge of the field. My shoulders slump. My heart sinks. I don't want to cause discourse. Not between any of the crew. But at the same time, irritation grates me like chalk on a board. Brooke's taken it too far if she's debriefed the crew on my sanity levels. I was *checked*, and I'm fine.

Leaves of the birch rustle as the breeze picks up, calming me and drawing my focus back to the work at hand. The not quite right-ness of the tree reveals itself when the leaves change rapidly from dark red to burnt orange to beige to dark green and back again. Nothing like this was reported back to The Company.

June lets out an audible gasp from where she's crouched a few feet away. In her hand rests a purple flower with bright white dots on its petals going from fresh to rotten to fresh again in seconds.

I kneel next to her, and we both stare at the flower. Fully bloomed. Fresh. Wilting. Dead. Blooming again. I brush a finger down the length of a petal asit repeats the cycle of decay and birth.

"What the fuck," Tomms' voice sounds from behind me. "What the *fuck* did I just watch?"

"The life cycle," I reply, in awe of the moment.

"No shit."

"What's going on?" Connelly asks as he joins us kneeling in the grass.

June nearly drops the flower, her hands shaking. "How is that possible?"

"Actually, it's dormancy," I say. I look back at the birch tree leaves. "Not the life cycle. Not truly. The same happened back on Earth. In the winter the plants decide to store all of their energy in the bulb in order to return in spring when the weather is more survivable. These plants seem to be rapidly cycling in and out of dormancy."

The real question is, what is causing the dormancy? What is the environmental trigger? Could it be Galactica's oxygen make up? The rotation around the sun?

My chest tightens as another thought occurs to me.

*What if the Hive rapid cycles too? What if there are dormant bees within it?*

"I can tell what you're thinking, Jensen," Connelly says. He shakes his head, slinging his gun around to hang from his shoulder strap.

I turn to him, scowling. "It might have the answers."

"If this shit—" he points at the wilted flower, "is what's happening to the Hive you can't go in it."

My cheeks burn and I grind my teeth. But instead of asking why not, I tell him as it is. "Last I checked, this is *my* mission. I'm going to get my answers. You can either come with me or not."

# 10

"Before we enter this hive, I want you to know that I will blame you forever if I die," Connelly says, his salacious voice tickling my ears as we cross the pollen lake. "Even if I'm burning in Hell I will curse your name."

"I thought this was part of your plan anyway," I say, careful to pace myself so I don't need to use the oxygen mask. "To convince me that the Hive is simply a coincidence?"

"No idea what you're talking about."

"You and Tomms," I say, my ears hot. "You told him you wanted to prove to me that the Hive isn't special."

His lips twist. "It isn't special. It's just here."

"*Okay.*" I re-focus on the Hive. "Whatever you say, sir."

"You should call me that more often," he says, his voice practically purring. "I like the way it sounds coming from you."

I suddenly become lightheaded, and I have to pause a second to steady myself. He *likes* it when I address him as an authority figure? There's something about that... I bite my lip softly and force myself to take another step forward without replying to him.

"Really, you should offer respect more," he says, his tone deepening. "It might get you to the places you want to go faster. As they say, a little respect goes a *long* way."

I clear my throat. "Noted."

Water laps at my thighs as we wade further in. It's light to the touch and oddly warm. If I stare too long it begins to shimmer. Brief and quick. Like light catching the top of a cresting wave. Bright then gone. There then not.

The air is thick and humid, wetting my skin and contributing to the discomfort growing over my body. I'm too flushed. I reach down and pull the oxygen mask to my face, taking in a deep breath of piercing cold air.

Connelly shoves past me in the water, pacing himself a few feet ahead. As he passes, he whispers, "Good girl."

Like I'm a dog. Like I'm doing something worth noting. *Like I'm his and he's impressed.*

I can't help the smile tugging on my lips as I tuck the oxygen mask away again. Maybe I should listen to orders more often. I'm grinning like a fool as we tread on, not stopping until the shadow of the Hive falls over us, encapsulating us in darkness.

I clutch my gun to my chest and take deep breaths as I take in the tall structure. The closeness solves a few more mysteries for me. Signs of decay surround the Hive. Beige gives way to gray color on the structure's walls, darkening where tunnels were built. A metallic rustic odor hits my nostrils, churning the contents of my stomach. Something dead lingers inside.

We pause at the base. There's an obvious entrance at the bottom, but there's something off about it. I squint and attempt to get closer, but Connelly throws out an arm to block me. He lifts a single finger in a clear command. *Wait.*

I fail to keep my exasperated sigh to myself.

His return glare is the second warning; I roll my eyes.

Still, I watch closely as he approaches the opening. He cocks his gun, as he takes the first steps through it. As his figure disappears, I inch closer. No way am I allowing him to clear the entire Hive by himself.

"Connelly," I say, hushed, into the yawning darkness as I draw close enough to peer inside.

There is nothing beyond pitch black darkness, but as I walk forward to enter the Hive, I hear a crunch. My foot rests upon the first step of a staircase. I move back into the water and crouch so I can get a better look at it. Dust flies into the air as I brush it off. Underneath the crust is wood. It appears human-made. My heart pounds as loud as thunder in my chest.

Light blinds me.

"Get in here, Jensen. You need to see this." He's here, shining a light in my face, and the next moment he's retreating further into the Hive.

*And I'm impulsive and irrational?*

I keep my gun ready, scanning the walls of the Hive as I ascend the stairs. The small flashlight attached to my black vest flickers on, lighting the path ahead. The stairs are narrow, bringing us up a floor or two into the Hive before releasing us into a large corridor.

The scent of rot hits me, and I try not to gag. Covering my nose with my shirt doesn't help, the stench is too overpowering. I bend over and throw up the contents in my stomach. In an instant, Connelly's hand is on my back, rubbing circles. He holds back my hair.

Once I'm done, I stagger backwards. My back hits the wall, and something thick drips onto my shoulder. I glance at it. Guts or slime, possibly. I try to move away, but I'm stuck. Connelly grabs my vest and tugs me away from the wall.

"What the hell is this shit?" he asks, his breath hot on my face as he tugs again.

I break free and slam into him, my hands splayed against his chest. Everything quiets in my head as I stare at him. My breath catches. His tongue darts out to wet his bottom lip; I want to taste it.

"Are you okay?" he whispers.

"Yes." A blush rises to my cheeks as I realize my breath probably smells like puke. I push away from him.

"Here," Connelly says, holding out his open hand, a mint resting in his palm.

I raise a brow as I take it from him. "You carry mints around?"

He smirks. "Not everyone likes the taste of an ashtray."

I pop it into my mouth, hoping my face isn't bright red at his insinuation.

Connelly gestures with his gun at the ceiling, leaning so his light illuminates the area above us. But the pit in the center of the room steals my attention from him, all embarrassment leaves my body as my scientist brain clicks on. I can hardly contain my excitement as I nearly skip toward the pool. Thrill spikes through my body as I approach.

A pool of slick honey rests undisturbed. It's fresh which means there must be bees here already, and they have to be alive. Somewhere.

"Connelly, do you know what this means?" I ask, my voice creeping up an octave. I pull out my sketch book from my pocket, scribbling down a description and shitty sketch of the corridor. "There's already a colony of bees on Galactica. There's hope. We can start the colonization of the humans immediately, I mean, *wow*, this is a breakthrough—"

"Jensen."

"I could use the hive for my bees," I ramble on. "Oh my god, this is perfect. It cuts the timeline at least in half."

"No, Jensen," his voice is short, curt, and hard.

I turn back to him. His face is dark and expression hardened. A frown creeps onto my face, and I tuck my notepad away.

"What?"

"Look," he says, taking the barrel of his gun under my chin to position my gaze upward.

Above us they rest.

Hundreds of eggs as big as my hand attached to the ceiling, stuck with honey. All of them connected by cords to a hole in the center, one that leads the central cord further into the Hive. A cursory glance around the room reveals no other passages other than the tunnels in the ceiling. My gut pressures me to climb, to search further in, to see if there is a queen at the center of the Hive. There has to be. How else would there be living eggs? Unless they're rapid cycling here too.

"Don't get too excited," Connelly says. "I'm pretty sure they're dead."

His expression is grim, dark eyes, searching. His body is still tense as if he perceives an unseen predator.

"What makes you say that?" I ask. Didn't he see the flowers? These eggs are alive too.

The pity is clear in his expression. "The stench."

"They're dormant. That's all." I take a step toward the honey. If I could just get a sample to compare it...

"I hope for your sake that they are dead." No mercy threads the tone of his voice. He means it.

"What an awful thing to say," I mutter, sticking my fingers into the golden liquid.

The shimmer inside of it is strange—not like the honey back on Earth at all.

"I would have to kill them."

Quickly, I turn on him, tears forming quickly. "You *can't,* Connelly."

"They're bigger than my head!" He takes a step back, and he laughs almost manically. "Think with that brain of yours for one minute. Normal eggs are almost invisible and they turn into bees the size of thumbnails. How large do you think these bees will end up? Your size? Bigger? Come on, Jensen. You're an intelligent woman. Put two and two together."

"Bees are not naturally predatory creatures. We have nothing to fear from them."

"Neither are humans yet we destroyed Earth with literal bombs."

He's right.

I blink away my tears, nodding in agreement even if I don't want to.

"I need to take samples," I say. I pull a few vials from my bag, and with careful hands, take samples from different areas of the room. I'll save the honey for last.

"What are you hoping to find?" he asks.

I shove a cork in a vial, sealing it as I think over what I want to share. "Well, clearly the Hive here has stood strong since my grandfather's mission. Perhaps even because it's man-made. There is much to learn about it: what makes it decay and revive at a slower rate, how the bees have managed to remain here—"

I stop myself before mentioning what happened to my father's crew. I am sure the Hive had something to do with it and I don't need to give any of the others more reason to worry about me. Although I can't help wondering if it's what drove him mad and if it'll do the same to me. Buzzing infiltrates my ears; I pause, standing at attention.

Behind the pool is a tunnel I didn't notice before. I swear it's just formed. Pieces of the Hive start peeling back, revealing a deeper room within. I impulsively following the buzz. It's calling me. My *grandfather's* calling me.

"Do you hear that?" I ask in no more than a whisper.

"No. What do you hear?"

I take another step, dropping my rifle, which slings against me on its strap. My vision shifts, blurring and bright orange hues glow around me like lightning bugs. A trail meant for me. Leading me to answers.

"Do you see that?"

Connelly hisses through his teeth, "See *what*, Jensen?"

"It's calling—"

He blocks my path, obscuring my view of the tunnel. I want to shove him aside, push past him, continue forth.

"Hey." He ducks his head, trying to make eye contact with me. "What are you doing?"

"I…" I blink several times, and the buzzing quiets in my head. "I don't know."

I hadn't realized the amount of sweat that pooled on the back of my neck, sliding down my back. Tingling sensations lick up my legs. It's too hot. Connelly mirrors my movements, still staying ready with a hand on the trigger though the gun is pointed toward the floor. He's ready for anything, but it doesn't make me feel safe. It makes me feel like prey.

"Let's report back," he suggests.

I don't want to go back. I want to explore more, discover if the eggs are alive or not. Maybe even find a reason to protect them. I want to find my grandfather.

"I want to go further in. Get more samples," I say.

His jaw clenches. "Tomorrow."

"But—"

"Tomorrow. That's an order." His voice is steady and low as he approaches me, narrowing the space between us until he's a breath away.

"You can't—"

He grabs my chin, rough at first before he lightens his touch, trailing his fingers from my chin to my neck. I make sure to keep my hand hidden behind my back.

"Listen to me," he says, leaning even closer. "Please, listen to me this one time, Jensen. Something's not right about the rot in this place, and you're acting strange—obsessive. I'm worried I can't protect you from yourself in here."

I tremble under his touch, wanting more, wanting to tilt my head back so our lips can brush against one another so I can reassure him that I'm fine. I lean in, and he takes a fast step away. He levels me with a singular disappointed look, like I've done something terribly wrong. And maybe I have, and if I haven't...maybe I was going to.

"Connelly—"

"We're going," he says, cutting me off. "Now."

"One last sample," I say, rushing toward the honey pool.

"No!" Connelly shouts, and suddenly his arms are wrapped around my waist and he tugs me toward the entrance we came from. "You don't need to bring *anything* else out of here."

"It's for science!" I claw at his hands.

He deposits me at the tunnel entrance, and I spin around to face him.

"You can't do this. It's not your call," I protest.

As I point a finger at him, he snatches my hand, pulling me toward him roughly. Our bodies are pressed so close together that I have to crane my neck back to peer at him.

His lip curls. "You will listen to me."

"And if I don't?" I ask, unable to help how my gaze dips to his lips and back up.

His pupils dilate, and his expression softens as does his grip on my hand. I use the opportunity and trail my fingers along his jawline. A shaky breath escapes him—I have him now. I shouldn't be thrilled to use our desires against him but...

"What will you do?" I whisper, standing on my toes to bring our faces closer together, leaning in so our lips are a breath apart. "Will you punish me?"

"Yes..." His eyelids sink, and I swear I can hear his heartbeat.

"How will you punish me?" I press my freehand against his thigh. "Tell me."

"I..."

I've never seen him so speechless; my manipulation is working. A little too well as an ache begins to build inside me too. I'm turning myself on thinking of ways that Connelly could punish me. An image of him pressing me up against the sticky wall of the Hive or shoving me under the pool of honey. His hand around my throat. Buzzing all around us.

He lifts a hand and brushes his thumb over my bottom lip. "I could never hurt you."

His words surprise me, and a small gasp leaves me. It must surprise him too because his nostrils flare, and he leans away from me, as if he caught himself in a trap.

I rush to keep him captured. "I appreciate how much you consider me."

"It's my job," he says, leaning back into me. I've got him again.

"Right," I say, smiling. "Because you're the '*get shit done*' guy."

He nods slowly. "Yes...I am."

"So..." I peer at the honey pool. "Let's get shit done and get out of here. Alright?"

I step away from him, wasting no time collecting my honey sample. When I return, he's still under my spell. I grab his hand, tugging him along the exit tunnel. For a second, I contemplate turning us back. I imagine I could get him further into the Hive, but I shouldn't press.

*You got what you came for today,* I remind myself. I will return to the Hive.

# 11

The air inside my tent is suffocating, but I'm reluctant to pin back one of the flaps. I don't want the crew spying on me or the five samples I collected. Connelly demanded I turn them over and wait until the Nectar lands to analyze. I won't be doing that.

I need to know more about them —I need to know more about the Hive *now.* The incessant buzz in my head won't leave me alone until I do. It begs, no, demands, to be heard. Harshly it pulses within me, enveloping me in a darkness only I can navigate.

Bright orange liquid dances in the beam of my flashlight. I turn the tube over, watching the honey trickle from one end of the vial to the other. It's beautiful, iridescent. My body comes to life at the sight of it, sending me tumbling down a hill of desire.

The radio crackles. I reluctantly set the vial down as I turn to the clunky machine next to my sleeping bag, my own personal station for reporting back to Brooke. Just another inconvenience I must suffer while on *my* mission.

A faint voice sounds through the static. I turn up the volume.

*"Come in, come in, Jensen."*

I pick up the receiver, pressing the talk button. "I'm here, Brooke."

*"Oh, good."*

I pinch the bridge of my nose as I practice my deep breathing. Just like the shrink told me to.

*"Talk to me,"* she says.

"Well, we've collected samples of the surrounding area," I say, and lay in my sleeping bag. We will be on this call longer than necessary, so I might as well get comfortable. "Galactica is exactly what they said it would be. It's a perfect place for my hives."

*"June reported that there was something strange going on with the local flora."*

"It's nothing to be worried about."

She pauses and asks, *"Are you 100% sure?"*

*No.* "Yes."

*"Okay."* There's almost thirty seconds of silence. *"We will land the Nectar tomorrow then."*

I'm surprised her interrogation is over. This battle was easily won. I should be elated, but something about it doesn't sit right with me. Brooke fights me on *everything.* Why is she not fighting me on this? I certainly can't ask her why without admitting I'm unsure myself, but I pocket the information for later.

"Great," I reply.

*"Expect us at zero four hundred hours,"* Captain Norman's voice filters over the radio. *"Copy?"*

"Copy that, Captain."

I'm not surprised he was listening. I dangle my receiver by

its cord, swinging it back and forth as I wait for the next command.

*"Let the rest of the crew know,"* Norman says. *"Over and out."*

I hang up the radio and scramble out of my tent. Tomms and June sit outside her tent, passing a cup back and forth. Connelly isn't with them, and from what I can tell, he isn't on the beach either.

"He went for a walk!" June shouts.

I frown and head toward them. "In the middle of the night?"

"Said he needed 'time to think,'" Tomms says in a mocking tone. He laughs. "He looked rather sad, actually."

I don't like that he's out there by himself. I wish he would have asked for company.

"Is there something you need, Jensen?" June asks.

"Oh." I gulp, quickly plastering on my most enthusiastic smile. "Captain Norman decided he will land the Nectar. ETA is zero four hundred hours, so we should be ready to receive them before daybreak."

"Fuck," Tomms groans. "That means no sleep."

"Great," June says, crossing her arms and jutting out her hip. "Thanks, Jensen."

I give a curt nod. "No problem."

I turn on my heel, but instead of returning to my tent, I creep toward the shore of the lake. In the distance, moonlight reflects off the watery pollen. I wonder if Connelly can see the moon from where he's walking.

*He's not yours to worry about, Hannah.*

I can't get tangled up in a relationship while I'm out here. I need to focus on my plan. Especially since it's coming together so beautifully.

"We're almost there, grandpa," I whisper into the dark of the night—my only friend on the planet.

# 12

The crew wastes no time unloading the Nectar after she lands. Despite our more comfortable bunks within the ship, Captain Norman demands we set up a fully functional camp between the forest and the lakeshore. 'Just in case someone gets left behind,' he said. I can't imagine what disaster would have to strike in order for Norman to leave someone on Galactica, but I get the unnerving sense that it's for me.

I eye the crew from where I stand on the loading dock. June and Tomms have been warming up to me, and I'm hopeful Norman will come around too. We've brought almost everything onto the beach now. Everything except my bees. They have to stay in the lab where they'll be safe with Brooke's research. I can hardly wait to start building their homes.

"It's warmer than I thought it would be," Norman says, his voice interrupting my thoughts as he trails down the ramp. He shrugs off his dark green jacket, slinging it over a shoulder as he runs a hand over his head. He looks back into the shadows of the ship—at Brooke.

She scrutinizes me. "Seems like the perfect place for a colonization effort to me."

I force a smile and tuck my hands into my back pockets.

"Galactica will be written down in history as the home of the bees," I retort. *Like it should have been before.*

"We'll see," she replies. She takes a step forward. "Your report on the structure was vague. Why is that?"

I knew she'd ask, but knowing and being prepared are two different things. Pins and needles creep into my stomach. "There's not much to report on it. It's decayed."

*Mostly.*

"Interesting," she replies. She shoves her hands into the pockets of her vest. "I do believe I'll have to take a look myself tomorrow."

"No," I nearly shout at her.

My face heats, and my hands tremble. Both Brooke and Norman stare at me, brows furrowed..

"I mean…" I wet my lips. "What I mean to say is that you should not go off alone." I force a tight lipped smile. "No one should go anywhere alone. Right, Captain?"

"Right…" Norman says, chuckling. He rests his hand on the back of his neck. "Besides, plenty of work to be done at camp tomorrow."

Brooke scoffs and turns on her heel back to the Nectar. I wonder if she's pissed that Norman took my side, but even more so, I wonder if she's touched my bees. Her and Norman were alone on the Nectar for nearly two days; plenty of time to sabotage my mission. My hands itch to check on the specimens, to ensure they're intact.

"Jensen, you should get back to work," Norman says. "Camp won't set itself up."

I nod with enthusiasm. I can't let Norman think I'm not a

team player. He's the only one that can pull the entire mission, so I need him to believe I can get along with the others just fine.

"Sorry, sir," I say. "I'm getting lost in thought."

He grabs me by the shoulder. I didn't realize how close we were standing until that moment. "You doing okay?"

"Why wouldn't I be?"

He studies me for a minute, peering into the depths of whatever soul I possess. It's a minute too long for comfort, and I start to wiggle out of his grasp. He holds on tighter.

"I know you don't know me very well and I know we haven't gotten off on the best foot, but you can lean on me if you need. Being so far out from home is not easy, especially for your first time. I know I was terrified my first time in atmosphere." His lips pull into a tight line before breaking out into an easy smile. "Be careful not to let that head of yours get *too* lost, and keep up on your medication regiment. Okay?"

"I appreciate it, but I'm fine. Seriously." I pointedly glance at where his hand is gripping my shoulder, a bit too tightly now. I wish he'd let go of me.

"Just trying to help, Jensen. You need to be careful." He eases off, allowing me to break free.

His warning flips a switch inside of me, and I shudder.

"Why do I need to be careful?"

"A wandering imagination can't be trusted in an alien environment," Norman replies.

I touch the oxygen pack attached to my hip, a smaller one that's easier to carry. "Connelly already took care of me in that regard."

He chuckles, his smile losing its luster. "It's not just the oxygen. People lose their minds on these sorts of missions for all kinds of reasons. Stick to the crew and you'll be fine."

The warning feels like a threat. I can't trust anyone here. I *am* on my own.

I think back to Connelly's words the other night. He's more than suspicious of the crew, even more so he's suspicious of The Company, and maybe that's something I should consider. Despite June, Tomms, and Norman finally giving me a break, maybe I *should* remain cautious.

I get back to work. Most of my supplies will remain in the lab, but I start to unload the boxes that don't need to be and set them beside my tent for safekeeping. As I carry my crates, I take note of everyone moving about the camp. They're all distracted by one another. I let the box in my hands thump to the ground. With a deep breath, I unlatch the crate, but before I can peer inside and take inventory, a shadow falls over its contents. .

"Need anything?" Connelly's voice filters down to me with a heavy scent of smoke.

What I want is for everyone to leave me alone so I can focus on my work here. I let out a frustrated noise, leaning back.

Connelly rests against a stack of crates, a cigarette hanging lamely from his lips. His hair is uncombed, and the breeze isn't doing it any favors, but still, in the bright morning light, he's gorgeous.

"Is there something *I* can help *you* with, Connelly?" I ask.

He playfully smirks at me. "Oh, no, I'm perfectly fine standing here watching you do your thing."

"And what is it specifically that you like watching?" I pull a stack of notebooks from my crate, tossing them into my tent onto my sleeping bag.

"The way you move about," he says.

I duck my head, hiding my blush as I return to the open crate. I remove a soft blanket to get access to the books under it; bound in worn leather, tattered from years of use. A layer of stubborn dust still clings to their covers after years spent tucked carefully under my bed back home.

"Some light reading?" Connelly asks.

I snort. "They're journals, but yes." I pause, reminded of his comment that he'd read about me. Smirking, I turn to him. "Don't you like to read?"

He pulls the cigarette from his lips. "Very much so."

My body thrums like an ignition switch was flipped.

"Do tell me what you like to read about." I set the journals on the top of another crate. My palms sweat as I wait for his answer.

He moves slowly through the sand until he's standing over me. His head blocks the sun from view, and flashes me that ever so lovely smile of his. My energy pulls toward him. A soft buzz sounds in the back of my mind. His hand brushes my waist.

"Everything I can get my hands on," he whispers. His pupils dilate.

I can't help shudder. "Everything?"

The Company does have a vast library of resources, mostly digital, but most of the community doesn't have a need to read beyond what their career requires. I find it hard to imagine Connelly spending hours lazed about a bed or a couch, nose buried in a book. He doesn't seem the type.

"I find that reading helps expand the imagination," he says. Now his hand is firmly resting on my waist. "Don't you?"

"I—"

"Connelly!" Norman shouts.

We separate, and I stumble backward, tucking my hair behind my ears. The sunlight is blinding without Connelly blocking it. In the distance Norman waves him over, and behind him stands Tomms, carrying what appears to be a heavy load.

"Break's over!" Norman shouts.

Connelly gives him a thumbs up before focusing back on me. He flicks out his cigarette, flashing me a large smile. "Catch you later, Jensen."

# 13

The campfire roars to life as Norman pours fuel into it; the rest of the crew let out a loud cheer. We're celebrating the official start of our mission. Or, we're *supposed* to be celebrating. I'm not. I sit at a table, passing the nearly full beer from hand to hand. I don't want to spend the night getting drunk and singing songs and bonding. I want to get to work.

Someone sits next to me. A lighter clicks, and Connelly takes in a long drag of a cigarette before offering it to me. I almost take it, only to see how he would react, but I shake my head.

He exhales a cloud of smoke which makes me wonder, would the smoke from our fire reach the bees if they were near the birches? Should I place the first colony farther away? Perhaps in the forest? Along the field on the other side of the woods? Inside the Hive?

"Stop thinking about work," Connelly says.

I set my beer on the table and focus on my boots sinking into the sand. "Am I so predictable?"

"Sort of," he says.

He throws a leg over the bench so he's straddling it. The cigarette hangs limply from his lips, and he reaches out and traces a line on my forehead. Heat creeps up my body.

"Your brows crease, and you get deep thinking lines here. Oh. Can't forget about the massive frown you get when you're problem solving." He chuckles as he withdraws from me. "You should think about getting a nicotine addiction. Might help alleviate the stress."

"I don't need another distraction." *Apart from you.*

He picks up my beer, swishing the liquid around inside. "Seems like you do since you're not utilizing your first choice."

"Who says beer is my first choice?" I ask, leaning toward him as I snatch it from his hand.

We're inches apart now, his breath caresses my face. I want to tease him the way he teases me. I want him to be nervous around me. To be on edge, cautious, curious, enticed.

"I might have other vices," I say, intentionally dragging my tongue across my bottom lip, daring him to do something.

The corner of his mouth twitches and he tosses the cigarette to the ground. He places his hands on the bench between us, using them to lean closer until our noses nearly brush. "Tell me about your other vices, Jensen. What really relaxes you?"

My heart pounds. The heat from my face dips to my belly and between my thighs as I think about what true stress relief would feel like. It's been a long time since I let myself have a taste of another, and for a moment my mind buzzes with the thought of being touched—of being stroked by a tongue as dirty as Connelly's.

"Perhaps I favor good company," I say.

I swear he lets out a small groan. "You wouldn't want the company of just anyone."

"No, I don't."

His breath warms my face, and I tilt my head back, just enough for our lips to brush.

"You're killing me..." He presses his forehead against mine. His hands find my thighs, and he digs his fingers into them. "Tell me you don't want this."

Someone clears their throat.

Connelly doesn't move. I lean back to see who lurks above. Tomms' wide eyes dart back and forth between us for a second before he clicks his tongue.

"What do you need?" Connelly asks through gritted teeth.

"Cigarette."

Tomms holds out his hand between us, wiggling his fingers which Connelly promptly smacks away.

"Don't you have spare packs in your bunk?"

"Nope! I get them from you."

"What about the ones you stole?"

"You calling me a thief, Connelly?"

Connelly reaches into his pocket with an overly-exaggerated sigh, pulling his pack out. "Fine. Here you go. Don't smoke them all in one place."

"Thanks," Tomms says, his smile faltering slightly. "Be careful with this one."

"Oh?"

He's clearly joking, but something about his unsure smile sets off warning bells in me. Do any of these people trust each other?

In a flash, Tomms is back in good spirits. "He'll turn you into an addict if you let him."

"That's a ridiculous accusation," Connelly says.

"I used to be *innocent* before meeting him."

"Innocent?" Connelly snorts. "You were smoking two

packs a day when I met you. If anything, your reliance on me has helped you slow down."

"It's okay. Admitting you have a problem is the first step," Tomms says, slapping Connelly's back. "I'm here for you, brother. Just let me know when—"

Connelly slugs Tomms right in the stomach. Tomms lets out something between a groan and a laugh and stumbles away. Connelly turns back to me, bright red in the face from laughter. I take a swing of my beer, too nervous around him to stay sober any longer. We *almost* kissed. He's going to distract me from my work. Uneasiness bleeds into me, and the buzz within my brain dies out completely, leaving me in silence.

*Relax.*

"Finally joining the fun, are we?" Connelly asks, pointing at the bottle in my hand.

I offer him my beer, and he takes a long drink until it's gone. He gets up to grab another one, and I watch him from where I sit. Three people have told me to be careful, but which of them meant well? The sure of himself captain? The comedic engineer with an addiction? Or the charismatic mission security officer who flirts? Which of them tells the truth?

Connelly is the only one that has wedged his way into my personal space. My thoughts spiral as I imagine the likelihood that he's lying to me. His smile is too open at times, and he's good at getting people to trust him—at getting me to trust him. Handsome and a charming personality make for a good cover in order to get close to me. The flirting is likely all a front.

I watch him as he grabs two beers from the cooler. My stomach twists as he flashes a smile at me. The enticing emotion I felt for him disappears in an instant as I conjure up every sinister reason he might have for toying with me.

Connelly is dangerous.

As he stops to talk to June on his return trip, I take the opportunity to save myself from his clutches. Cool night air hits my face as I retreat across the camp to where I belong. Alone in my tent with only my dark ambitions as company.

# 14

Colonizing an entire planet takes a great deal of effort. All of the *right* conditions must be met in order for nature to support human life, but The Company rarely cares about what nature or the planet itself wants. Most of the human colonies on planets are manufactured and in doing so, The Company destroys the planet. They see it as a success because they profit from it, but it was a complete failure on humanity's part.

He let it be known through his research that he disagreed with the fundamental values, or lack thereof, of The Company. It wasn't so obvious in the way radical groups held protests. No, he was quite crafty in expressing his beliefs. The average person might overlook his subtle comments in his research, but I never did. I could always read between the lines—he *hated* what The Company was forcing him to do. His dreams were bigger, better than anything The Company would ever allow, and it destroyed his sense of self to know that he would never be more than a tool to them.

Perhaps his despair pushed him too far and drove him to insanity. Maybe his quiet anger boiled over into a sea of mistakes that led to the end of his life. Or for all we know The Company got tired of his politics and ensured he would *never* come back from Galactica.

Whatever the reason, I am going to discover the truth of what happened and restore our family's good name.

"What made you pick this spot?" June asks from where she's perched in a tree to my right. She volunteered to help me build the hives—a welcome hand, honestly, and better than asking Brooke to assist. I'm still hesitant to accept that the help is out of a purely good heart, but I do believe June is warming up to me. Besides, hiking up to the orchard with all of my supplies would have taken twice as long without her help.

"Bees need a nurturing environment like humans," I explain. "This location provides shelter, sun, and a nearby water source."

"Do you really think they'll hatch?"

"If everything goes correctly, yes."

I brace myself on the ladder. Beads of sweat coat June's forehead, her hands move slow and steady as she places another layer of wax over her hive. Traditionally, a hive box would consist of seven layers in the Langstroth style. I reject tradition and defy expectation. My hives will be hanging from trees like wasp nests to protect them from predators.

Wasps—such volatile creatures. Much like Brooke, and perhaps, like Connelly too. He's unnerved me for days now with his constant lingering like my shadow. Even the thought of Connelly bothers me. The insistent need to know what he is doing here eats away at me and consumes my every thought. What's his real purpose? Because I am sure he's not here to protect us from threats that could be lurking on Galactica. *Is* he protecting them from me? And if not me, then who?

A soft chill spreads over my back despite the temperature, and I have to steady myself against the trunk of the tree I'm in.?

*Focus, Hannah.* I touch my bottle of meds through my pants, I don't need it. I don't. Not yet. I swallow. *No, I'm fine.*

I wipe the sweat off of my brow. I want to ask June, but I know I won't get a different answer than Tomms gave me: mission security hired by The Company. I cast a furtive glance at her. She has her black hair tied up similar to mine. Her lips are pinched and she's squinting through the daylight to see the knot she is working on.

*Maybe they're in on whatever he's doing.*

She raises an eyebrow and frowns. "Are you feeling okay? You look pale."

Panic begins to bubble up like a fountain inside of me. My hands scramble for my pill bottle, and I pop open the lid, dry-swallowing my meds. I force myself to take a deep breath.

"F-fine," I stutter.

We climb down our ladders, moving on to configure the next hives a few trees down. I remain silent, turning over questions in my mind as an attempt to calm myself.

"What's the deal with you and Connelly?" June asks, climbing up the next tree.

I falter for a moment, caught off guard by her question. "Uh... What do you mean?"

"I overheard him and Tomms talking the other night. It sounded like you two..."

"Nothing happened," I say a little too quickly.

"Hmph, I thought you liked him, considering all that time you spend together," June said with a tone of doubt.

"What? No. I don't like Connelly... He's Connelly," I say, doing a poor job of recovering from my first misstep. I take a deep breath and regain my composure as I settle my ladder against another tree. I'm not sure how much I can trust June, but I decide to try my luck anyway. "What do you know about him anyway? I mean, other than the military commander thing."

"Not much, why do you ask?"

"I'm just curious," I say, holding up the supplies she'll need.

June hesitates mid-reach. A smirk slowly climbs its way onto her lips and her brows shoot up. With the way the sunlight brightens her beige skin, she looks like an amused god staring down at me.

"Curious in what way?" she asks, not containing her own curiosity very well at all.

"Um..." My stomach flips and fills with butterflies and a blush rises on my cheeks. The buzzing grows louder in my head. "He's just... interesting. I want to know more about who he is."

She grabs the supplies from me, but lingers. A strand of hair falls into her face. "You *do* like him!"

"No!"

She laughs. "You do!"

"Shhh!" I wave my hands at her then cover my face. It's my fault for asking and insinuating, and I hate that she knows the *wrong* thing about him. I don't like him. I can't like him. Not if he's here to watch me.

"Please don't tell anyone," I say in hopes that she'll really believe I have a stupid crush.

She grins at me as she reaches her hand up and across her lips like a zipper, locking away the secret and throwing out the key. "Your secret is safe with me."

Relief floods me. "Thank you."

Static crackles in the air, pulling both of our attention to the radio perched on a supply box a few trees down. Brooke's voice is nothing more than a barely heard whisper from our vantage point.

"I got it," I say to June, waving her off to keep working.

I trek toward the radio, taking my time to get to what is sure to be another annoying check in. I shove my hands in my pockets, observing the way the sunlight hits the field. In the distance the top of the Hive peeks over the treeline. My chest tightens, and the warm air suffocates me as my gaze lingers too long on the object of my desire.

"Come in—come in—" Brooke's voice crackles.

I pick up the radio and punch the comm button. "What do you want?"

More static, then, "That was not a polite way to address your supervisor, Jensen." She sighs. "I want a report on your progress. You've been up there for hours."

"Two hives are established," I report. "We started off slow but the pace is picking up now."

"Do you need me to come up there and help?"

"No." I grind my teeth together. "We will be back before dusk."

"Great," she says. "Don't tire yourself too much. We need to catalog all of the specimens tonight before light's out."

"What? Why?" I shake my head. "They're frozen. Do you think they've multiplied or something?"

There's a moment of silence over the radio before her irritating voice comes back on.

"It's protocol."

*Right. Protocol. How could I forget?* I resist the urge to be sarcastic with her. She knows best, she always has. I'm just... here.

"Over and out," she says.

I don't bother to respond, slamming the radio down on the

supply boxes. I'm supposed to be having the time of my life setting up the initial stages of my dream experiment. Instead, I'm paranoid about a potential malignant spy who I can't seem to stay away from and anxiously irritated over my worst enemy who can't seem to stay away from me. I run my hand over my face, letting out a deep groan. Reluctantly, I get back to work—the only distraction I have from my spiraling thoughts.

At the end of the first day, we set up ten hives in total. Five hanging from trees, five on the ground. My back aches, and my breath remains short. I'm proud of our work. The hives are spread evenly throughout the grove. My only wish is that there were more flowers close by other than the ones sprouting from the bottom of the birchwoods.

A whistle rings in the air. It's one of the others, most likely Connelly, signaling that we need to get back to camp. I imagine Brooke sent him even though we're all aware we must return before nightfall. God forbid we wander around at night. *For safety,* Connelly says, but I think he's full of shit. It's so he can get sleep at night and not have to worry about me trekking out to the Hive.

"Jensen! June!" Connelly yells.

I brush my fingers over the hive in front of me one last time. My body demands to remain out here as the sun goes down, to feel the warmth drain from the air, to see the stars blink to life one by one. Slowly, I tilt my head back, basking in the last rays of the day. They burn against my cheeks. Is this the same warmth my grandfather felt on his face years ago? Did he enjoy it as much as I am? What was his last sunset like?

"Come on," June says, breaking me away from my thoughts. "Let's go before he drags us back."

Reluctantly, I collect my belongings—a pack filled with supplies and tools. I tug it onto my shoulders, hiking back down the slope. Connelly waits for us in the distance. Alone, though I'm not surprised. The others must be preparing supper.

My boots dig into the dirt as we join Connelly. I don't bother greeting him or pausing to acknowledge his presence. I blow right past him and head toward camp. June's pace puts her ahead of us by three meters, but she keeps checking on us and giggling. Her discretion is laughable. So much for keeping it a secret.

For a second I think Connelly is purposely walking slower to accompany me because he's somehow found out about my fake crush. Even though that makes no sense, I'm on edge about it anyway. Maybe it wasn't a good idea to ask June my questions.

"You're quiet lately," he says.

I let out a half-hearted laugh. "Yeah?"

"It worries me," he admits.

My gut twists—he's *worried* about me. I grind my teeth together, ignoring the way my heart buzzes with delight at this new information. I should be annoyed that he's so worried because that means he's going to keep hovering.

He matches my pace so we walk side by side. He softly coughs and says, "I worry about you."

"I heard you the first time."

"Oh."

He makes no further comments as we head into the dark of the forest. Cutting through the trees is the quickest way to the beach that we've found. For the first few days we stayed closer to the open field, but after determining that there were no predators in the woods, we made the shortcut. Laziness continues even on planetary expeditions.

"Have you always wanted to work with bees?" he asks.

"Yes."

"Never thought of doing *anything* else with your life?" he asks, lighting a cigarette. "Not even for a brief moment? A rebellious year or two?"

"Nope," I say. "You?"

He only chuckles, and it's the most brilliant sound in the world. I dare a glance at him. His auburn hair falls onto his forehead, and his cigarette rests gently between his lips. I imagine those lips being put to use somewhere else.

*No, think of something else, anything else.* I try to brush the dirty thoughts from my mind, but they overwhelm me like a swarm of bees.

*Stop it, Hannah. He's a distraction.*

"I'm more of a vagrant myself," he says, flashing his pearly whites. "I love to take odd jobs that lead me to interesting places."

I wonder what interesting places we could journey to together.

*No. Think about the hibernation patterns here. It's warm right now, but will the bees be able to warm themselves when a storm comes? Would it better serve me to share a tent with Connelly should dangerous weather occur?*

My foot kicks something hard, and I pivot forward. Big arms wrap around me, yanking me back to a standing position before my face hits the dirt. My heart pounds, and I brush off my jumpsuit as I step away from my savior. But he moves close to me again and places a hand on my waist.

"You good?"

I swallow. "Yes. Perfectly fine."

His fingers caress my chin, but I don't look at him until he forces me to. "You sure?"

I nod as much as I can with him holding my chin. He leans close, and the scent of smoke hits my nostrils despite the cigarette abandoned on the ground. His lips curl into a cocky grin, and it's then that I notice the stubble on his chin. He's usually freshly shaved. He must have skipped it this morning. My lips part as my eyes drift over the slope of his nose. He's handsome. Does he know it? It certainly seems like he does.

He brushes his knuckles against my cheek in one slow motion that sends chills down my spine. I press my palm flat against his chest. The black fabric of his t-shirt feels wrong against my hand. I want to be touching his bare skin, digging my nails into his flesh.

The hand holding my chin shifts, tangling itself in my hair. I like that better, especially when he tugs it so my head is tilted back. The pain is delicious.

Connelly closes the space between us, brushing the tip of his nose against mine. I try to close the distance between our lips, but he pulls away, only slightly. A whimper leaves me. I want him.

"Why am I so drawn to you?" I whisper, barely able to breathe.

He shakes his head. "I have no idea, but…"

I don't give him the chance to answer. I slide a hand up his throat and around the back of his neck, pulling him against me as our lips crush together. His tongue parts mine, and I let out a soft moan. He tastes sweeter than honey. I waste no time losing myself in him.

"Jensen…" he whispers against my lips.

Heat floods my entire being at the sound of my name on his tongue. I want more, no *need* more. I bite down on his bottom lip, he groans in response. It's then that I remember where we are and that June is only a few meters ahead of us. I realize I'm *kissing* Connelly—a man I'm not sure is here for the right reasons, who might be here to tear down my guard.

I pull away as much as I can, but he grips me hard. I can't help the piercing flood of emotions that threaten to overwhelm me. Warning alarms scream all over my body, and a wave of blistering lightning pulses through me. This is what everyone wants—they want me to mess up.

"We can't do this," I force out, and it sounds weak even as I say it.

His brows furrow. "Why?"

"Because it's a bad idea. You're nothing more than a distraction." I blink away tears that spring to life in exchange for the best glare I can muster. "This was a mistake. It shouldn't have happened."

He lets go of me, stumbling backward as if I've slapped him. "Right." His expression grows blank as he slips on his cool mask of indifference. "You're right. I'm sorry."

Even though Connelly continues on the path to camp, I can't help deflating at the idea that he can so easily walk away from me. I trace my lips with my fingertips, wondering if his ease is proof enough that it's all an act to get under my skin.

# 15

On the morning of the first hatch, I fly out of my sleeping bag. It takes little effort to tug on my jumpsuit, unzip my tent, and announce to the group that I'm heading to the fields. I take only my gun and the vial of honey I took from the Hive with me. I need nothing else but to see the bees—to feel their souls connecting to mine. My body fills with the thrill of anticipation as I rush out of our camp and on to the trail.

I break into a light jog, ignoring the commotion breaking out behind me. It doesn't matter who is assigned as my guard dog today. All that matters right now is ensuring that the bees are waking up. I pump my legs faster, practically sprinting through the woods. My calves start cramping and stitches form in my sides, burning builds in my lungs.

The forest is dark. Twigs snap beneath my feet. Movement parallel to the trail creeps into my periphery, but I ignore it. The bees are more important. They're the only thing that matters to me now—completing the first step of following in my grandfather's footsteps. The bees will lead me to him.

Behind me someone shouts, but I ignore them. I fly through the woods and break into the field. Seconds pass before I'm on my knees, completely enraptured by the sight. Through the hexagonal cells I can see them moving. Some of them are small honey bees, others are larger drones, and there at the very center rests the queen of this hive. She twitches in her sleep.

*They're alive.*

"They're alive!" I scream, a sob of joy ripping from me.

I can't pull my attention from the bees in front of me. One of them crawls out. It's *so* small. It shouldn't be ready to fly yet. In a perfect world a worker bee would be helping feed this bee, keeping them in place until they're ready to work for the queen. But all they have is me, so I reach my hand in, letting the small insect crawl up my index finger.

I pull out the vial of honey. I place a single drop on my finger and the bee drinks the droplet.

"Jensen," a breathless voice sounds from behind me. Connelly crouches next to me. Even with him next to me, my mind stays connected to the bee. His hand touches my shoulder lightly but I'm not pulled to him like I usually am.

It crawls along my knuckles, and I swear my heart swarms in a scattered song akin to hope. For the first time in my life I feel purposeful. This is what I am meant to do. The keeper of bees. The savior of humanity.

"Isn't it beautiful?" I whisper. "Such a small part of life, and yet so important. All that power in one little insect."

"You can't run off like that," Connelly says.

"A miracle of life..." I whisper, still so entranced. I can barely comprehend what he's saying to me.

"It's dangerous out here," he continues. "Norman and Tomms discovered something in the woods this morning—" He sighs. Suddenly, he's jerking my shoulders and forcing me to come face to face with him. "You aren't listening to me. There's something *alive* in the forest."

The bee flies off my finger, and my stomach sinks.

"What do you mean?" I ask.

Connelly's eyes darken. "This thing is probably what killed your bees, Jensen. We don't know what else it might do. Norman has ordered us all back to the Nectar for a briefing."

*Killed my bees?*

A lump forms in my throat. Most of the hives have been pulled from the trees. The ones on the ground are completely destroyed. In my excitement I located the only intact box. The rest are simply gone.

Darkness descends upon me, and I am frozen in place. I swallow back my cry of agony, blink away tears. How could this have happened? Who could have done this? *What* could have done this? Fire burns within me, and I ball my hands into fists.

"We have to go *now*," Connelly says, rising to his feet and pulling me with him.

I nod, but I'm already thinking about checking the rest of the boxes. It's stupid, but I can't help myself. I need to know if any of the other bees lived. I move toward the next tree, and Connelly grabs my arm hard enough to bruise.

"I need to see if any of the others are alive," I whisper. My body trembles before him. He's seeing me so weak, so feeble. Grief and anger have nearly overtaken me. I know there's nothing left of this young colony, but I need to see to be sure that hope is lost.

I need to see that I've failed.

"Please," I beg.

Connelly's lips pull tight, but he lets go of my arm. His decision confuses me as much as it excites me. My mouth opens and closes several times before I get the words I want to say out, "Thank you." I nearly fall to my knees. "Oh, thank you."

"Just be quick," he grunts out, cocking his gun. "Okay?"

"You don't have to stay. I can handle myself." I motion toward my own weapon. "You should go back to the Nectar."

He closes the distance between us, hard metal of his gun brushing against my bare arm, making the hair stand on end. My throat dries, and I make a poor attempt at swallowing as I lift my gaze to meet his. Warmth radiates off of him, pressing into me like a forcefield. His free hand lingers near my waist, as if he can't decide whether or not to touch me. I lean toward him, instinctively, wondering if he will put his rough hands on me again. I hope he does.

He levels me with a single look, one that threatens and thrills. "I'm staying. That's final. Got it?"

I have no choice but to say, "Yes, sir."

"Good girl."

He takes position standing guard without another word. There's nothing to argue. Even with his back turned, I stare at him, perplexed. If he was working against me then it would be easy to leave me out here at the mercy of the mysterious forest beast. I would die out here, and no one would know. Through his black shirt I can see his body tense. He scans the field, proving that he's protecting me. Why did I ever doubt that he was protecting me? Why did I push him away?

Without thought I reach out and tug his shirt. He turns, and I pull him close. I raise a single brow, forgetting what we're out here for and becoming totally entranced by his piercing eyes. I need the truth.

"You care about me," I say.

His brows furrow. "Is that a problem?"

"It wasn't a mistake to you—the *kiss* wasn't a lie." My heart buzzes. He did kiss me back, and he *wants* me now.

He nods slowly, and it's all the confirmation I need.

There is no place for shock as I collide with him. He does

not hesitate either, dropping his gun in favor of pulling me into his arms, tangling his hand in my curls. The kiss is sloppy, reckless, and at the same time, despite all logic, perfect.

His tongue parts my lips, and I tilt my head to give him better access. This is how we're meant to be—entangled with no reservation. All of the truth lingering between us like the expanse of space, infinite and yet not close enough. He walks us backward, pressing me into a tree as he hoists me up. My legs wrap around his hips, finding pleasure in the hardness he presses against me. I grind into him, letting a small whimpering noise escape me. He grins against my mouth.

He tugs at my shirt until it untucks itself, then his rough palm is pressed against my stomach, trailing up. He barely grazes my breast and I moan. My body demands release, and I want Connelly to give it to me. He responds in earnest, tugging my belt loose. We separate only long enough for him to release me of my pants, and suddenly he's on his knees.

There's nothing gentle about the way he takes me with his mouth. His tongue undoes me, and he matches his pace with two fingers pushing in and out. I can't help the soul-wrenching moan that leaves me. He works faster, building me slowly toward release. It's as if the stars exist behind my eyelids. Nothing has ever felt more right than this—than him.

"Beg for it," he demands, slowing his touch.

I gasp, looking down at him. My hands are tangled in his curls, holding him close to me. His face is red. His heavy breaths hit my center, coiling tension tighter. I need him to keep going, but I can't—

"Ask for what you want, Jensen," he says.

I twist my fingers tighter in his hair, yanking his head back.

"Please," I say, "finish what you started."

I can hardly believe the heady demand of my own voice, but he obeys, dipping his head back down to drag his tongue along my center. My eyes flutter shut, and I relax into him. Dark sounds unfurl in the depths of my mind as Connelly brings me up, up, up. A roar of small little wingbeats covers the sounds of my moans, or perhaps they accompany it. I am barely breathing as heat bursts through me. I'm so—

Growling in the distance breaks us from the moment, pulling us apart. Connelly's head snaps to the side, searching for something. He stands slowly, grabbing his gun. I pull up my pants and buckle my belt as spikes of cold rush through me. All is quiet except that dark growling.

"What is it?" I whisper.

"Shh," he commands, holding up a finger to silence me as he takes a tentative step toward the sound.

I pick up my pack and sling it over my shoulder. I brush my fingers through my hair, scanning the treeline. Trampling sounds echo across the field like ravenous thunder. All my breath leaves me.

We're not safe out here. Our eyes meet at the same time something bursts forth from the woods.

"Run," Connelly demands.

I take off toward my right at full speed, shedding my pack, but my rifle gets caught in it and tumbles to the ground with it. Pops of bullets sound behind me. Too far behind me. I chance a glance over my shoulder.

Connelly isn't following me. He's facing down the creature.

I slow, screaming back at him. "Connelly! What the fuck are you doing?!"

"Move your ass, Jensen!" he yells.

He walks backward, keeping focus on the creature that is now approaching at a slower pace. My gun is halfway between Connelly and myself, and I'm not the only one to notice. The creature turns, frothing at the mouth as it stares at me.

The creature appears to be a deformed bear. Antennae protrude from its partially exposed skull—part fur, part bone, part skin. The legs are insect-like, and I don't understand how it can carry its body weight. Two large wings protrude from its back. It moves quickly, and it is clearly capable of complex thought as it appears to pause and think, like it is calculating how fast it can reach and kill me.

But there's something else about it—the eyes. They're almost...human.

"Don't. Move."

Connelly's command strikes fear in my body. I've made a grave mistake stopping, one that might cost both our lives. I'm weaponless, and I can't outrun the creature either.

"I'm going to draw its attention to me," Connelly yells. "Once I do, run as fast as you can and don't look back."

"Cause that sounds like the ideal plan," I mutter under my breath.

I don't pull my gaze away from the creature as it stalks through the grass. My heart nearly beats out of my chest, and my palms grow sweaty. I might throw up. Connelly shootst at it again, walking *toward* it instead of away from it.

As if on cue, the creature returns its focus to Connelly. I should run, but I can't. Connelly is too close to the creature, and he's going to run out of rounds before he can escape. We both know it. He'll die if I don't do something. But what can I do? True fear bubbles inside of me, and finally, I stop thinking. I only act.

I race forward, diving for my rifle. In one not-so-smooth roll, I grab it up and mount it in the grass. My belly presses into rocks in the dirt, but I grind my teeth and line up my sights. A red dot hits the body of the creature, and I take one steadying breath. I'm only going to get one chance at this.

*Pop. Pop. Pop.*

The creature charges at me.

"What are you doing?" Connelly screams.

"Shut up and run!"

"I'm not doing that!" He runs toward me.

He won't reach me before the beast does. I turn my attention back to the creature, preparing myself for killing it.

*'Kill or be killed,'* is what grandfather used to tell me as he stood behind me while I aimed. *'When the moment comes, you don't hesitate, Hannah, not even for a second. You put that beast down without mercy. Learn to do that and you might just be able to kill a man when the time comes.'*

I was shooting a deer that time, and not even a real deer but an automated one. That's all we had on the ships at the time. This is *much* different.

"Jensen!" Connelly screams.

The creature is barreling toward me, and its humanness sickens me.

"Fuck," I breath out.

*Focus.*

I let off another round and the bullets bury themselves in the beast's side. Still it charges me and lunges, casting a shadow over me. I prepare to meet my end. It was worth it, if only to save Connelly. I take a deep breath, but nothing happens. A ricochet of gunshots goes off, accompanied by a loud earth rumbling crash. I find the creature dead before me.

I search for my savior only to find Norman and Tomms approaching from one side and Connelly from the other.

"You idiots," Tomms laughs. He shakes his head as he pokes the creature with the tip of his gun. "Definitely dead." He looks pointedly at me. "You're welcome."

I launch myself into Connelly's arms. He holds me close, cupping the back of my head as I bury my face in his neck. All of the tension in my body releases at once, and it's better than any he could have brought me to. He's safe. He's alive. We both are, and I've never been more grateful. I let stinging tears fall down my cheeks.

"We're safe," he whispers, wiping away my tears. "I've got you."

Connelly and I break apart but not before he plants the softest kiss on my forehead, a gesture that buries itself deep in my heart. I search his face, attempting to memorize every freckle and line. He's genuine. I can trust him.

"Again, you're welcome. Good thing we heard all your shouting," Tomms exclaims, interrupting our moment. "Shit, you'd think we'd get a thank you for saving their lives."

"The only thing that matters is they're safe," Norman says. He scans the forest in the distance and runs a hand over his head. When he turns, all of the assuredness of a captain in charge reflects back to us. "Let's get you both back to the Nectar and have Dr. Keller examine you."

Without resistance, I follow, grateful to be alive.

# 16

Steamy air hits my lungs, suffocating me as I inch into the shower room. Water like rain penetrates my ears. Someone else is in here. I hesitate at the threshold, listening for any indication of who it might be.

Norman and Tomms headed back to the bridge, Brooke should've already showered today, and June was still in the bunks. Deep inside me a pulse thrums, and my gut twists. *He* is here.

I trip over my own feet, catching myself against the wall. He's already staring at me. My gaze dips, and my mind reels. He's only wearing a towel wrapped tightly around his waist, leaving the rest of him exposed. My belly tenses as I scan over his chest, freckled and muscular.

"Don't be a stranger, Jensen," Connelly says, his lips tugging upward.

I wet mine as he moves closer, like a predator stalking his prey. I'm frozen in place. All I can do is helplessly watch. My heart thunders faster. Everything slows.

"Like what you see?" he asks.

"I..." I'm at a loss for words, and my face heats. *Of course* I like what I see. I love what I see. I *want* what I see.

Dark desire webs out from my center, and finally, after what feels like a millennia, take a step forward. Fire lights through my chest, encapsulating my heart and bringing me burning confidence. I meet him halfway between the running shower and the door, dropping my fresh clothing on the wet floor. He raises a brow, and I set my jaw.

His gaze trails over me. "Need any help?"

"No," I say. I tug my shirt up and over my head, tossing it aside before slipping out of my pants. My undergarments aren't very flattering, but you wouldn't be able to tell with the way Connelly's eyes darken and his lips part. He's drinking me in.

He reaches out and brushes a thumb along the waistline of my panties. My breath hitches, and I decide to move past him. Before I can get around him, he grabs my arm, tugging me close.

"Jensen..." His voice is dark and sultry. He *wants* me. "I think it's far past time to finish what we started, don't you?"

"Yes." I let out a shaky breath, leaning into his warmth to steady me. "Let's finish it."

He wastes no time bridging the gap between our lips. He trails soft kisses against my jaw, and I tilt my head back, giving him access to my neck. Against my skin he lets out a soft breath, chilling me. I dig my fingers into his sides, and he tugs me closer. One hand wraps around my waist, walking us toward the shower. The other tangles in my curls.

"I've waited so long for this," he whispers against my neck. "You have no idea how many times..."

He chuckles, pulling away as we reach the running shower. As he opens the glass door he runs his gaze over me again. I am naked under his gaze, and that's when I realize I still need to shed the rest of my clothes. I laugh at myself, reaching behind me to unclip my bra.

"Wait," he commands.

I pause as he rounds me so he's behind me. His warm hands touch my back softly, and he pulls the clasp free. With a tenderness only a lover could have, he tugs the cloth free from my body, trailing the tips of his fingers down my arms. A tight coil winds itself in my center, and I lean into him, wanting to savor this moment—wanting to savor his touch, him. Everything quiets, and I feel an indescribable steadiness in his arms.

"Is this okay?" he asks as his hands slip down to my hips.

"Y-yes," I stutter out.

I can barely comprehend words. All tension leaves my body. My mind grows blank as he tugs off my panties, leading me into the shower. I barely register that he dropped his towel as I watch the water wash over him. His wet hair appears brown, and my heart skips a beat when he runs a hand through it, pushing it back across his skull.

He offers me his hand, and I take it, joining him under the hot droplets. My eyelids flutter shut as I let the heat of the water consume my being. Decay and fear wash away with the dirt. Connelly's calloused hands drift up and down my arms, never straying without permission. His fingers linger on my collarbone, and when I peek up at him I'm hit with desperation.

"Your beauty is infectious," he whispers.

Our eyes lock, and I close the distance between us once more. A desperate need to taste him fills me, and I take his lips in mine. He presses against me, digging his nails into my back. I let out a soft cry. He takes the opportunity to move from my mouth to my neck, planting harsh kisses against it.

The water falling on us is warm and sweet like honey, and I'm fully captivated in the moment.

He walks me backward until my back is pressed against the shower's cold glass door. Icy pain shoots over me, but it mixes with the pleasure of his relentless tongue on my skin. He lifts my leg, bracing it against his hip as he drags a knuckle along my center. A gasp leaves my lips.

"Relax," he commands.

I obey. I wrap my arms around his neck, bringing him as close as I can. Between us, his tip presses into my wetness, and I jerk my hips toward him.

"Tell me how much you want me," I whisper because I need to know. I *have* to know that this is real.

He lets out a chuckle, and with one thrust he fills me. "Can't you tell?"

My only response is a moan. He's staring at me, his eyes wide as saucers and as beautiful as the stars.

"Yes, but—"

"But nothing, Jensen," he says, kissing me softly. "I want *you,* and I want you *right now.*"

Soft buzzing infiltrates my mind as he continues to deepen our kiss, and my heart tightens. I shouldn't give into this—into him. It's a distraction, it's.... All is lost as he pulls out and thrusts back into me. I lose myself to the rhythm of his strokes as he brings me closer and closer to the edge. I spin out of control—flashes of brightness cloud my mind, and I hear nothing but the sound of my soul as I crash into him, exploding like a supernova. The buzzing seems to align with the only word my heart knows. *Connelly.*

# 17

The med bay is cramped with all six of us packed in, but the secure room was the obvious choice for our debriefing after the attack because only a crew member's fingerprint can unlock the doors, nothing gets in, nothing gets out. The Nectar reassures us that we are safe as long as we are with her, but I'm not delusional enough to believe it like the rest of the crew. I've never been safe in my life—except when I'm wrapped up in Connelly. I cast a sidelong glance toward him. He's across the bay, leaning against the wall with Tomms. It takes no effort to conjure up the image of him taking me in the shower, and my body floods with desire at the memory. Not even an hour later and I'm already hungry for him again.

"Nectar, are all monitoring systems online?" Norman asks. The stress apparent in his voice is enough to break my concentration on Connelly. I look at our captain from where I perch on the exam table next to June and my stomach rolls. Norman's expression is buggy and sweat gathers at the base of his neck as he swivels on his heel to pace back and forth.

Yes. All systems are online.

"Good," Norman replies. "Alert us if there's any movement."

Affirmative.

"Are you sure it was a bear?" Brooke asks. Brooke lingers near the door, her back facing us as she stares out into the hallway of the Nectar.

Norman redirects the question to me.

*Why is he asking me and not Connelly?*

I peer between Norman and Brooke, taking a sharp breath to calm the spikes protruding from my chest. Once more, I'm tense, but I can't let that show. I recall the memory of the bear-like-creature. It was humanoid in some aspects, completely alien in others. But, I can't tell them of my suspicions of where it came from without sounding insane.

"No," I admit, settling for a partial truth.

I'm not sure of anything anymore except that we're not safe on Galactica. Not like we thought we were; not like my grandfather theorized we would be. I try to make sense of what I saw.

"So are we totally fucked or what?" Tomms asks.

Norman glares at him with a laser focus. "Do you think that is an appropriate question given the circumstances?"

Tomms' brows furrow. "Um, yeah." He spreads out his arms. "We're in a metal box on a planet that has monsters. What's not appropriate about asking if we are fucked or not?"

"You need better phrasing," June says. Her calm demeanor is contagious, putting me at ease when I am sitting next to her. "You might have asked, 'What do we do now, Captain?'"

Tomms parrots June's question, his voice high-pitched. *"What do we do now, Captain?"*

"I..." Norman tilts his head back, clucking his tongue. "I don't know."

"See!" Tomms points. "We're fucked."

"That is not what I said," Norman snaps. "What I do know is that we are in a situation that has developed factors we can no longer anticipate. We need a new protocol."

"Seriously? Are you *fucking* serious?"

"Will you stop cursing?" Norman asks. "Your attitude is not appreciated nor helpful."

Tomms slumps against the wall, giving up. I understand his frustration. We all want answers, but I also know that we won't get them easily.

Brooke crosses the room, drawing everyone's attention.

"I want to dissect the creature," she says.

We fall into an uneasy silence. Dissect the creature? She's insane. We don't have the kind of equipment necessary to examine it safely. An intelligent person would wonder if its deformities were caused by an infection, or perhaps radiation —some malfunction that we could inherit should we continue to be exposed. The situation calls for quarantine, not dissection. What is she doing?

"Would that provide valuable insight?" Norman asks.

Tomms bursts into laughter. "Oh, so we're all delusional now. Cool." He gets up. "I'm done with this debriefing. Let me know if anyone suggests something sane as a solution."

He walks out of the med bay, and Connelly follows, sparing me a warning look as if to say *stay right there.* As if I'd consider going anywhere else under the circumstances.

"I believe The Company would be interested in knowing there is life on Galactica," Brooke says. "The creature is worth documenting and studying. Perhaps we might even discover others of its kind."

Norman pauses to consider it, but ultimately he shakes his head. "No, it's not safe. We're going to pack up and start departure procedures immediately."

*"No."*

Brooke, Norman, and June stare at me. Blushing, I bite my lip, rocking on my feet. I wipe my sweaty hands on my pants. Pounding rings in my ears, and I'm not sure if it's my heart or the planet screaming at me. All I know is that we can't leave yet. Not until I can get back in the Hive and find out for sure what happened. I have too many questions that need answers.

"Jensen?" Norman asks, raising a brow.

I brush my hair from my face, tucking it behind my ears. I say the only thing I can, "The Company sent us here to begin the process of colonizing Galactica, and I assume you want a paycheck. You won't get one until we've done what we came to do."

"You set up the hives. Our work is done," he says.

"No, it's not." I lick my lips. "The creature destroyed most of the specimens. We're not even close to completing the mission."

"How do we deal with the unknown dangers?" he questions.

I shrug. Protection is entirely out of my skill set. That's Connelly's job, and he's not here to chime in. I can only hope Norman feels enough pressure to complete the mission, or at least that Connelly was right—that they really, deeply care about money and reputation. That's what I need to push.

"Every mission is dangerous, Captain," I say. "The question is, how badly do you want to prove your worth as a crew?"

His jaw drops slightly. I shouldn't have struck so low. Why did I strike so low? My breathing quickens. I tap the side of my leg.

"Additionally, my research is far from over," Brooke interjects. "I am The Company representative here, and I happen to agree with Dr. Jensen's directive."

"You want me to stall departure and risk everyone's lives?" Norman asks, exasperated. "The Company wouldn't want that. You can't tell me they would."

*Oh, you have no idea.*

"Besides, it is *my* decision," Norman states, gruffly.

I pinch the inside of my elbow, waiting on Brooke's reply.

"I am sure upon hearing of your bravery The Company will give you a bonus," Brooke says. "Is that not incentive enough?"

"Well, I mean...I..." Norman pinches the bridge of his nose. *"Fine* but we sleep on the Nectar at night." He looks me dead in the eye. "You have one week to re-establish those colonies. After that, we leave. And if there's even *one* more incident before then, we leave. Got it?"

"Yes, sir," I say. I should be happy to get another chance with the bees, but my stomach twists in knots. I don't have enough specimens to create even half of what I already lost. And there is so much I still need to find out.

"I will head out to the field with you tomorrow, Dr. Jensen," Brooke says. "I'll perform my dissection of the creature there while you tend to your bees. I do believe you should ask for additional assistance in re-establishing your colonies since you will need to work quicker than before."

An idea I hate even more than sleeping on the Nectar—asking for help, but I nod agreement. Dealing with Brooke is a small concession if it means I have another chance at saving the bees. Another chance at exploring the Hive.

"I'm happy to help again," June volunteers. "I'm sure Tomms would too."

"Thank you," I reply.

"Great." With a grunt, Brooke departs from the room with Norman following.

I let out an exaggerated sigh. I have no idea how I'm going to help the bees grow at a faster rate. It's pointless to try. Disappointment floods me. My grandfather wouldn't have given up so easily, what he wanted to do was too important. He would have stopped at nothing to make life-saving medicine with the bees. He was ambitious and confident.

But I'm not like him. I'm not brave or strong. I can't keep up with the lies. They're consuming me. I'll have to tell *someone* the truth of why I'm here.

"What's wrong?"

I jump at the sound of June's voice. I'd forgotten that she lingered behind. She's red nosed and puffy faced and her lips rest in a pout. Somewhere in that conversation I missed when June got upset. Then again, maybe she's just tired and panicked. I know I am.

"Oh, um." I try to relax my shoulders but fail miserably. "Just anxious, I suppose. It's a lot of pressure to set up all those hives again, especially with fewer bees."

"And our lives are on the line," she adds.

"No kidding," I say. I pause. "I hope nothing tears these hives apart. I wish we had better materials to make them stronger."

She nods, casting her gaze away from me. "You know, there is a place we could get inspiration from."

"Yeah?"

I'm almost nervous asking it, and my heartbeat quickens as she paces toward the door, pausing once she reaches it.

"The Hive."

Of course. It's the simplest answer, and it gets me where I want to go. But there's no way.

"Connelly will never approve of me going by myself," I say.

She raises a brow. "Who says you'd go alone?"

"Who would go with me?"

"I would."

Slowly, like a sneaky minx, June smiles. I reflect the expression back to her, my body filling with a deep thrum. The idea of visiting the Hive is enticing, and sneaking out to go is even more so. I can get my answers without Connelly hovering over me, *and* I can save the bees.

"We would have to keep it to ourselves," I say, quietly. "Connelly can't know."

"Midnight then?" she asks, one hand on the door handle. She's ready to leave.

"Midnight."

# 18

Night-vision goggles bring everything into focus. I adjust them on my head, careful not to get my curls caught in the straps. A sinister chill hangs in the air. It's not until we approach the pollen lake that I notice the low-hanging fog creeping around our ankles and following us to the Hive.

I attempt to explain my experience with the Hive to June, but my voice wavers and my hands shake. Strange doesn't begin to cover it, and by the time I'm done, June merely shrugs. She's not fazed by any of it—she's brave, or stupid. Either way, she needs to be prepared.

As we approach the Hive, I slow. There is a slight green-blue glow to the Hive at night. It should look wrong to me, but it doesn't. It gives off a familial sense that feels like home. Like I'll be comforted the moment I enter.

"Why is it glowing?" June asks.

"I don't know," I say, "but I think we're going to find out."

We make the trek up the stairs, entering into the center chamber of the Hive. The room with the honey pool is different this time. Amber liquid drips from the ceiling, and a sweet scent hits my nostrils. I hold up my hand in a fist, forcing June to linger in the entryway as I investigate the room.

*Oh.*

There's no eggs on the ceiling, not any whole ones, at least. Some are gone entirely, and others have cut themselves open like a peeled fruit. In the distance is the faint sound of wings. I let out a small breath as pins stab my stomach. I was right about the rapid cycling. The specimens Connelly thought were dead *are* alive. And they're still in the Hive.

A bright flash catches my eye. It came from a tunnel across the honey pool. I motion for June to join me.

"Did you see that?" I whisper, pointing toward the light's origin.

"Yeah," she replies. "I thought there wasn't anything here."

"There's not supposed to be."

I walk forward, fearful that we have to trek through the liquid until June points out a narrow footpath along the outer wall. We take it with my lead. Behind me, June's breathing intensifies to match my own. With every step I grow more light headed, and I wish I remembered to grab my meds.

Bile forms an immovable wedge in my throat. I don't know whether or not I should be afraid of the possibility of my grandfather's survival or not. He's a monster I've been told to be terrified of, but he's also the only person who ever cared about my safety.

We close the distance between us and the flash, but when we enter the next room, there's nothing there. I lower my gun with a long breath of relief. The room is empty, and the buzzing has gotten farther away. There's not going to be anything useful here. I stifle the frustrated noise that attempts to escape me. It's an empty, decayed beehive. That's all.

"Jensen?"

June's crouched in a corner, pulling something out from the wall—a red backpack I recognize. If I am right about who that backpack belonged to, I can't let her see the contents

"Are you going to help me?" June asks, letting out a frustrated noise.

I drop to my knees, grab a strap and yank. It takes our combined strength to pull the bag from its place. The backpack lands in my lap. June raises a brow at me, clearly waiting for me to open it. I do, and what I find inside isn't so strange—supplies, water, a notebook. Without thinking, I snatch the notebook and stand. June occupies herself with the rest of the bag's contents and doesn't seem to mind when I back away a few steps.

The notebook confirms the worst of the worst. It's his handwriting inside. My grandfather has been inside the Hive.

"Oh, look at this!" June says. She's holding a jar of long black needle-like objects.

Bee stingers. I swallow and shove the notebook into my vest and return to June, ready to caution her as she twists open the lid. Before I can say anything, June pulls one out.

"Fuck," she curses, dropping the entire jar. It shatters on impact.

I'm frozen in place, watching from outside of my body as she holds up her now bleeding finger. The stingers are larger than life in comparison to the bees I was supposed to breed. A thin trail of blood runs down her finger. We both stare at it, entranced.

She's hurt. We should leave.

I'm about to say so but a thump behind us causes both of us to nearly jump out of our skin.

"What was that?" June asks.

"I…" I consider telling her I don't know, but that wouldn't be true. I have some guesses.

I motion for her to stand. "Come on. Let's go."

"What—" Her question turns into a scream.

All the air leaves my lungs as I view what's behind us. Standing there is a creature more horrifying than the bear-creature. This one is humanoid yet an insect in every way that matters. Large wings carry it toward us. I make contact with its human-like eyes—eyes that remind me of my grand-father's.

It stops and backs away. Everything slows and it's like I'm moving through jelly as I reach toward the large bee-man.

"Don't!" June screams, jumping in front of me.

The creature hisses, rearing back before lunging at June. I am frozen as its pincher latches onto her arm, wrenching her back and forth. Her screams flood my system, overstimulating me. I'm overwhelmed, hot, terrified. Fear pulses through me.

*What am I doing?*

I shake my head and level my gun at the creature.

"Let her go!" I yell, as if it can understand me. I can't kill it. It's the discovery of the century. It's full of life, and even if it's a violent life, it's still worth saving. Tears stream down my face at my indecision, at my internal conflict. I didn't feel this way about the bear-creature, but for some reason *this* thing has meaning to me.

June cries in pain as she kicks at the creature. It pins her to the ground. Honey covers her as she sinks into the floor. The creature's thorax flexes and brings its stinger down into June's belly.

I pull the trigger.

Ringing fills my ears, but the creature backs off. I don't waste time pulling June to her feet, pushing her out into the room with the honey pool. She takes off into a limping sprint. I follow, not daring to look behind me as it chases us. It's closing in on me, the flap of its wings, the hiss of its breath, the buzzing. The ever-present, haunting buzzing.

Terror thrums through me. June's almost through the honey-room, and I'm right on her heels. I trip.

My heart nearly stops. The creature lingers on the other side of the pool, watching me. It tilts its head back and forth as if it's curious. A thread of familiarity pulls taut between us. The distinct knowing thrum drawing me in. Its dark stare peers deep into my soul like it recognizes me too, like it misses me.

*Does it recognize me?*

I'm ripped into reality by June grabbing my hand and dragging me after her. I remember nothing but her hands purging my desires, trapping me with her as we leave the Hive. I hate her. Even as we splash into the safety of the pollen lake. Even as we shed our gear. Even as the buzzing stops completely.

"What the fuck was that, Jensen?" June shrieks at me once we're safe. "What was that thing?"

I'm sobbing but I don't understand why. All I feel is a cavernous emptiness.

I try to remember every detail of the creature we encountered.

"We have to alert the Nectar," June says.

"No!" Before I can stop myself, I tackle her to the ground.

We both breathe heavy, my hands around her windpipe and her clawing at me, thrashing to get out from under me. But I'm not suffocating her yet. I don't *want* to kill June, but I can't let her expose the Hive for what it is. Not now. Not when I'm starting to understand what my grandfather saw in this place. The Hive is no longer glowing. Instead, it stands out like a dark thumb against the horizon.

"No," I say again. "You will tell no one about the creature."

I ease up enough for her to speak.

"You're going to let it kill us?"

"No, I won't." I pinch my lips together, thinking it over. "No one goes inside the Hive anyway. We're safe. Let me have some time."

"Or what?"

I squeeze her throat, and she spits in my face. All I see is red. "If you tell them about the creature then I will tell them about your sting."

"What?"

"You were stung by the creature," I growl. "Quarantine protocol would have you left behind on this planet in case you're infected."

June sneers. "Norman would never leave me here."

"Are you sure about that?" I ask, cocking my head to the side. "Because a week isn't long enough to find out what that sting will do to you. The protocol is thirty days in isolation. You really want to find out whether or not you're worth it?"

Her lip trembles.

I ease up on my grip. "Do we have an agreement?"

"Y-yes," she croaks out. "Please don't tell them about the sting."

"You keep my secret, and I'll keep yours," I promise, pushing away from her. She rubs her throat as she glares at me from the water. From here on out, I need to watch her closely.

# 19

The last slide of frozen bees stares back at me. Fate rests between their black and yellow stripes; these tiny bees are their species' last chance at survival. They're the last chance I will ever have to redeem my grandfather's name and prove to The Company that his research *had* meaning. He wasn't some crazed lunatic who made bio-weapons for no reason. His medicinal research must have gone awry. I *know* he didn't mean to make super-wasps. He wanted to make enlarged honeybees because their production levels would be greater.

And I want to do the same—to do what he could not and engineer medicinal bees to help cure people. But if these bees fail, it will mean that I have failed him. I tremble at the thought, because these bees are not like the others. Their thoraxes are too long and the antennae spaced too far apart. I've seen this species before, but I can't place it.

*It's not possible.* I packed the specimens myself. There were no other species among them, and all of the specimens were in perfect condition upon departure from The Company. I rub my eyes, hoping that it will make the bees appear normal, but they're not.

*Fuck.*

My grandfather would not have panicked in my shoes. He would have been inquisitive. I bite my lip so hard blood pools in my mouth. I fight the rising panic, scrambling for my medications. I'm only *seeing* something different. They have to be the same. There is no way for them to be different. It's obvious—I'm too overworked, too tired, and now I'm hallucinating differences because my anxiety wants to torture me.

I down the medication, swishing it back with large gulps of water. The coolness of my palm on my warm forehead is soothing while I wait for the meds to kick in and slow my heartrate. Any minute now. Then I can get back to work.

Brooke waltzes into the sterilization chamber and waits for the gas to dissipate before striding through the automatic door.

"Sorry I was late," Brooke says. "I was tending to June in the Med Bay."

I tense. "Is she sick again?"

Coldly, Brooke replies with a curt, "Yes."

She crosses to her station and pulls out a rack of her miracle serum. The blue liquid splashes in their vials.

"When would you like to head out to the field?" Brooke asks. "For the bear?"

"Oh," I say, placing a steadying hand on my chest. "You were serious about dissecting it?"

"Yes? Why would I joke?"

"I...I..." I finish with a shrug because there's no reason.

"Exactly," she says with a huff. "I wouldn't pass on the opportunity to study an alien lifeform, and besides, I want to be the one to name it."

I don't mean to be annoying, but I'm going to do it anyway. "Doesn't that honor go to the person who discovered it?"

Her face twists.

"So, Norman or Tomms should be the one to name it." I don't dare suggest I have a say in naming it, even though I was part of that discovery.

Brooke returns to her experiment. "Bold of you to assume I wouldn't take credit for the discovery with The Company anyway."

"You would do that?" Shock floods my voice.

"As if *you* wouldn't?"

Her disgust for me is palpable, and I grimace. The comment takes me back to the fight we had all those years ago.

"Come on, Hannah," she says with a laugh. "We both know you believe in group projects."

My cheeks burn, and I ball my hands into fists. The stinging in my eyes won't go away no matter how much I blink. I shouldn't have let her upset me. But there's no defense for what I did to her. The university might have excused my plagiarism as a snap in judgment due to mental illness, but that isn't the truth. The truth is that I stole our dissertation and published it as my own so I could get funding for my post-grad research. It was selfish.

"Whatever," Brooke says, throwing up her hands. "Believe what you want to believe."

"Why does it matter anymore?" I ask. "What is the point in ruminating on the past? You got your promotion. You have an amazing career."

"Yes, I do," she says as she carries a stack of trays across the lab. She stops at my table. "I may have found my way out and into the life I wanted, but that does not change the fact that you destroyed me."

"I—"

"And you didn't even apologize for it," she snarls.

The lump in my throat becomes impossible to swallow as I stare at her. The hurt is clear across her face.

"I'm sorry, Brooke," I whisper. "But you have to understand, my grandfather—"

"No." She drops the trays. They clang as they hit the ground and scatter under tables. "Apologize without justification! That lunatic—"

"He is *not* a lunatic." I stand slowly, grabbing my pants and twisting the fabric between my fingers.

Her lip curls. "All you have ever cared about is proving that he was innocent. Did you ever stop to think about why that matters so much to you?"

"He's my grandfather."

"He's gone, Hannah!" she screams, a single tear rolls down her cheek. "You chose a dead man over your friend. You chose redemption of a failed scientist over moving on. And what has that gotten you? You have no friends, no family, and everyone at The Company thinks you're a joke."

I break. Sobs wrack my body, and I stumble backward, tripping over a metal stool. My back hits the ground hard, knocking the wind from my lungs. Brooke's face neutralizes before hard expression replaces it.

I shake my head. "That's not true." I'm weak even saying it.

"Oh yeah?" she asks. "Who's left? Connelly? You think he actually gives a damn about you? "

"He does," I grit out. Lightheadedness washes over me as I get back to my feet. I need to stabilize soon. "He cares about me."

Brooke laughs. "That's rich. That no good dog is here to keep an eye on you, nothing more. Don't get it twisted." She picks up her trays and heads toward the exit. "You should watch your back, Jensen."

My breaths shorten. Could she be right? Is my trust in Connelly misplaced? Has he fooled me so easily?

*No. She's only trying to get under your skin. She's only jealous of you.* I run myself through my truths.

With great effort, my body comes back online; all of my doubt is replaced by pure rage. I glance at Brooke's work station, fixating on the vials of blue she left sitting around. A single one of those would solve all of my problems, and with the way she was so needlessly cruel, she'd deserve it.

The doors open again. I tense, expecting to see Brooke's seething face. Instead, it's Connelly, grin and all. I force a smile, but deep down I'm frightened with Brooke's warning fresh in my mind. As he approaches, his grin slips away.

"What's wrong?" A crease forms between his brows.

"Nothing." I shake my head, wiping away any remnants of my tears.

He scoffs and rounds the table until he's right next to me. Slowly, he pulls me into his arms, and all my emotions rise to the surface. Fresh tears fall down my cheeks.

"Tell me what happened," he whispers, kissing the top of my head softly.

I open my mouth to spill my guts, but I hesitate. I can't tell him about my conversation with Brooke. Not yet. Not now. I'm reminded again how much I don't know about him. I might know his body, but I have no idea what secrets lurk within. Brooke *could* be right.

Instead, I push away from him. "I don't want to talk about it."

I could tell him. I *could.* He's nothing to worry about. He's just...Connelly.

*But is he?*

I swallow, turning back to the table. "Is there a reason you stopped by the lab?"

"Do I need a reason outside of wanting to see you?" he asks.

"No, but..." I gesture at the experiment set up before me. "I'm busy."

He reaches out and grabs my hand, planting a kiss on my knuckles. "Even too busy for me?"

"Connelly..." I frown and pull my hand away. A pit opens in my stomach. I can't be around him now. "I think..." I suck in a breath. "We need to talk about what happened."

He pulls back, straightening. All of his joy is stolen, and I can tell that he knows I'm about to put up a wall. His jaw clenches, and he looks away from me.

"What about it?" His tone shifts, like he's digging claws into me.

"Norman's new timeline puts a lot of pressure on me," I say, quickly, trying to justify it in any way that makes sense. "I need space."

"Space." He laughs but it's gloomy and harsh. "Are you serious right now?"

I flinch. "We need to be professional, so I can focus."

"I thought you knew me better than to think I'd distract you from the bees," he says, plainly disappointed.

Connelly is right. I do know that. He's been nothing but supportive, protective, loving even. But I don't know if any of what we had was real anymore.

"Please," I say, desperation creeping into my voice. "I like you, I do, but this is really important to me. It's my grandfather's legacy at stake—my whole career. You have to understand that."

"I do understand it," he growls. "What I don't understand is how you can stand there and believe I would hurt your reputation."

"I'm in charge of the mission. Our relationship is unprofessional at best, unethical at worst." I hate the words the minute they leave my mouth, but I have to say them. I can't risk it if Brooke was telling the truth. "I...*This* needs to end for now. Maybe once we're back home..."

The coldness reflected in his stare is enough to stab me in the heart. I'm gutted, but I can't take my words back now.

"You got it, *boss.*" He takes a step back as he salutes me.

Everything in me cracks open as he turns on his heel and leaves the room.

# 20

"How did you manage this?" Brooke asks.

Numbness envelopes me as I turn to face her—my enemy, or perhaps now, my savior for telling me about Connelly. Upon my finger crawls a single bee that's three times the size it should be and will continue to grow even larger. An impossibility of nature. Despite the fact that I don't understand this miracle, I can't help but feel a swell of pride grow in my chest. *I* did this.

"No idea," I reply. "It's a miracle of nature."

"A miracle?" Brooke asks in her usual mocking tone. "It's scientifically impossible that they have matured so fast in only four days."

"Ah shit, Keller, lay off. It's fucking amazing," Tomms says. He leans forward and pats my shoulder. "Congratulations. You must be stoked."

One by one the entire crew begins a cycle of praise. Everyone wants a turn letting the bee crawl over their hand. But there's only one person's approval that I don't hear, and it's the approval I seek most. Connelly raises a single brow, his lips pulled tight. I wish I could read his mind, to know what he thinks of this development.

Connelly lights a cigarette. He takes a long drag before finally speaking.

"Good job," he says, blandly. Not a hint of warmth in his voice, but no one else seems to notice. "Never doubted you for a second."

"Thank you," I whisper back. *I'm sorry.*

"I might have doubted you slightly," Tomms says, smirking. He approaches the open bee box, crouching low. "But these things are seriously—*ouch!*"

Tomms withdraws his hand, sticking his index finger in his mouth. I watch as he suckles on the site of the sting. The bee that stung Tomms flies away rather than dying—an anomaly. Without alerting the group, I kneel next to Tomms, picking up another bee from its sanctuary.

I squint. This *isn't* a figment of my imagination. I took double the dose of my medications this morning to be sure I wouldn't see anything like I did in the lab when I thought the bees moved. No, what I'm seeing right now is true. These aren't the docile bees I brought with us to Galactica.

Honey bees aren't hairy, but these ones are, and the abdomen and thorax are connected by a slight, distinct waist. I can think of only one explanation for these strange bees: they're half wasp. But that's not possible unless...

I suck in a breath as the bee on my hand injects venom under my skin. Like Tomms' bee, it flies away. I watch it go and it occurs to me—I've somehow created a modern mutation. I have walked the footsteps of my grandfather without even trying.

Tomms clears his throat. "Um—"

"Do *not* tell us you're allergic to bees right now, Tomms," Connelly jokes.

"None of us are," I say, ignoring the sinking feeling in my belly. Is this the same mistake my grandfather made out here? Did he mutate another species of bees by accident?

"I think they are targeting us," Brooke says, tracking a bee flying close to her face.

"The bees?" Tomms asks.

No reply was needed as her observation proved to be true less than a heartbeat later. Bees swarm from their nests, hundreds of them taking flight. I swallow, and slowly stand, backing away from the nearest hive. The buzzing of their wings is a song of anger, of viciousness. They *are* hunting us. Don't they know I'm their creator? Don't they know I'm on their side?

Connelly cocks his gun behind me. It'll do absolutely nothing. They're bees—not bears, not the creature in the Hive.

"Jensen, get behind me," he commands.

But I don't want to hide from them. In fact, I want to get closer to the bees, to show them that we're not the threat they perceive us to be. I want them to know that I'd never hurt them or betray their trust. I'm *here* for them.

The hives continue to combine, swarming into a large dark cloud over the birchwoods. They climb higher and higher in the sky, forming odd shapes like clouds. Deep within me a delight awakens. Thick saliva pools in my mouth. I want to join the chorus of their buzzing bodies.

As I move forward, Connelly barks an order at me.

I'm entranced, addicted, utterly taken with the formation of the bees. Their whirring becomes a song of pleading—asking if they can take all of us, asking me to join them. I *should* join them. I belong with them.

"Shit," Connelly curses.

"What the fuck is she doing?" Tomms asks. "Jesus fucking—"

"Do not finish that sentence," Norman snaps. "The Nectar. Everyone. *Now.*"

Someone tugs my arm nearly out of its socket, dragging me along. I dig my heels into the dirt. I can't go with them. Not now. The bees pulse toward us, curiously seeking, chasing, hunting us.

"Jensen, don't make me—"

"Connelly!" Norman's sharp bark floods my hearing. "Tighten up!"

"You heard the man," Connelly says. He steps in front of me, and before I can say anything, I'm over his shoulder.

We break into a light jog. It's all Connelly can do while carrying me. Somehow he still manages to pass both Brooke and Tomms on his way down the slope toward the Nectar. Thankfully, I get a clear view of the cloud of bees the entire way back, expanding and shrinking like a thumping heartbeat.

The rest of the crew is cursing and complaining as they rush down the hill. I let out a soft whimper as we reach the pollen lake shore, returning to the safety of the Nectar. The bees do not follow us. Instead, they travel over the pollen and toward the Hive, disappearing into her rotted holes. The Nectar swallows us; I've never felt more lonely than when Connelly drags me into her metal protection. I don't belong here with them, I belong out there, with the bees, in the Hive —with my grandfather.

# 21

Buzzing swells in my ears. Humidity soaks me through, but it's warm inside the hive and easy to get lost inside its nearly identical golden tunnels.

*Where is everyone?*

I set foot through an archway and encounter a scene I am not ready for. Breath leaves my lungs. Moans and laughter penetrate my ears. June is on her knees, face pressed into the ground as Tomms hovers over her, his fingers deep inside her, pumping in and out. Her soft moans become music to my ears. Brooke kneels on her other side, her face flush with color as she watches. I lick my lips, my heart pulsing in rhythm with my center.

Tomms notices me first. A grin appears on his face, he holds his hand out for me to take, gesturing for me to join them. It's depraved, and I shouldn't, but—a body presses into me from behind.

"Join us," Connelly commands.

His fingertips trail along my collarbone until he reaches my shoulder, tugging down on my shirt. His touch is euphoric. His breath hits the back of my neck as he chuckles, but he releases me and goes to join the rest of the crew. I stumble after him, enraptured in the haze of their desire. My gaze flickers between all four of them. Slowly, my body succumbs until I am kneeling in front of Connelly.

My vision blurs as he cups my chin. He's never seemed so delicious before. I want to consume him like honey.

He leans forward, brushing his lips against mine. "You are wearing far too much."

"Do you want—"

"Yes." He cuts me off, helping me out of my vest and jacket. Rough hands run along my arms until they hit my waistband. He tugs at my belt, and my weapons drop to the ground. I'm at his mercy now that I am bare before him.

I press my hands against his chest, daring to remember the sculptured structure of his form. He is everything.

"Tell me how to pleasure you," he whispers, walking his fingers down over my breasts, my abdomen, and lower. "I want to hear you whimper my name."

I could already be whimpering and I wouldn't know it. I throw myself at him, the heat bubbling up inside as I paw at him. He chuckles, turning me so my back presses against his front. One of his arms wraps firmly around my waist, holding me against him, his free hand roams up my thigh. I lean my head back, relishing his touch.

Another hand, colder, brushes against my breast. Brooke is leaning into me, into *us* as she flicks my exposed nipple. She takes my flesh into her mouth at the same time Connelly presses his finger against my clit. Pleasure erupts from my center, and a tight coil forms within me. They've timed themselves perfectly, as if they discussed it.

"More," I moan. "I need more."

"So impatient," Connelly chuckles.

Brooke bites down, and I hiss in pain or pleasure—I'm not sure anymore. I'm lost in them. Brooke's hands are callused, her fingers join Connelly's, parting my lips, entering me in even strokes. Behind them, June is spread out before Tomms, moaning louder and louder.

My ecstasy builds slowly. I don't want it to end. I'm not even sure what we're *doing* anymore. All I know is that it feels good. Too good. *So* damn good.

"I want to taste you," comes Connelly's voice, and suddenly I'm on my back.

*Brooke holds her down as I drag my tongue up the center of her perfect folds. She's so sweet on my tongue like pure honey, and I want more, more of her like this. I never want to let her go, ever. She is everything.*

My body spikes with endorphins, and my hips buck. His breathy laugh floats up to me, and he blows cool air onto my center. It's *exactly* what I want, what I need. He anticipates me more than anyone else.

Connelly's hands drift up my abdomen and over my breasts, where he pinches my nipples.

"You taste like heaven," he whispers. He pulls away slightly, his hand disappearing somewhere behind him. Then he's drizzling honey along my stomach, over my breasts. His tongue follows the trail, sucking tenderly on each nipple. The touch of his tongue elicits a sharp moan from me. I can hardly breathe. I'm trembling, and I'm about to—

*I watch Connelly as he moves to kiss Hannah. Their lips lock together, and a pulsating sensation burns my desire hotter. They are gods in this Hive, two masterful bees—queens of the colony. If they wanted, they could devour and tear each other apart.*

*I lay still, utterly entranced by their union. A warm hand, belonging to Tomms, brushes down my abdomen, and I realize I'm not the only one watching them with awe. June and Tomms pause their activity to watch Hannah and Connelly together. We're all hearing the same call.*

Finally, we break away from one another, and we all move into action. Hands and lips and laughter fills the space. We're all tangled together, one body, *one mind—*

"Oh, for fuck's sake!"

My eyes snap open. I'm naked, tangled up in sheets on my bunk.

"Put your clothes on! Now, Jensen. That's an order," Captain Norman barks while covering his face.

My commanding officer just walked in on me masturbating. My cheeks burn hot as I tug up my pants.

*What the fuck just happened?*

I tie up my hair as I think. This isn't a common side effect of my medication, so something else must be wrong with me. I am warm, but not fevering.

"Are you clothed yet?" Norman asks.

"Yes, sir."

He lowers his hands. "Come to the bridge. We have a situation."

He turns on his heel, forcing me to follow after him.

"What sort of situation?"

I can hear it all in the strained sound of his voice. "Let's just say you are not the only one who has descended into... inappropriate ideations."

Anxious energy claws its way up my chest and into my face. "Inappropriate *what*, sir?"

"Do not make me repeat myself."

I shut my mouth. I'm not the only one acting out then. If more of the crew are giving into sexual acts without provocation then something is wrong with all of us. A pathogen of unknown origin. An infection caused by something we ate.

I swallow hard as we enter the bridge and my mind wraps around an absurd thought.

*It's a mating call.*

# 22

"How many of you have been stung?" Norman asks after I pitched my theory: my mutated bees, which have interacted with all of us, might be the cause of the 'hallucinatory horniness' as he calls it. A cabin-fever-like pathogen spreads through the venom of their sting, which makes us want to mate with one another, to repopulate.

*"Well?"* he prompts us again, waving his hand in the air.

Solemnly, I raise my hand and dare a peek at the others. None of us can meet each other's eye, but everyone raises their hands. June's head is bent, cheeks bright red, and Tomms can hardly keep his gaze still. Brooke sits straight up in her chair, arms crossed with her bottom lip curled in disgust.

Only Connelly appears to be comfortable. He has a hungry look on his face as he stares at me, a longing clear across his face. I want to go to him, to fling myself across the table and into his arms. I grip the edge of my seat. Norman clears his throat, rather loudly, preventing me from acting on my impulse.

*We're infected,* I tell myself. *Definitely infected.*

"Great, I'm the only one not stung then." Norman lets out a long sigh, running his hand down his face in an exaggerated manner that annoys me. His attention, unsurprisingly, locks onto me. "What do we do, Dr. Jensen?"

"I..." I lick my lips, stalling.

What do I really know of pathogens? Or infections? Or even hallucinations? I'd know more if I could just get my thoughts to slow down. How did this even happen? The bees were *normal.* They shouldn't have mutated. I didn't do anything differently, so what's wrong with them? *I can do this. I only have to breathe. In, out.*

I rest my forehead against my hand. It's burning hot. Even my thoughts begin to jumble, and memories of my grandfather start to warp into terrifying images of bees and body parts and—

I take a deep breath and glance at Brooke. *She* would know what to do.

"Dr. Keller, any suggestions?" I ask.

She crosses her arms over her chest. "Seriously? Bees are *your* jurisdiction."

I try not to let my nervous impulse to laugh out loud take over. "Yes, well, I am asking for assistance, so if you can—"

"Are you trying to insinuate that you are not the proper party to find a solution to a problem in which you caused?" Brooke challenges me, tilting her head to the side. "Come on, Jensen. Tell us what you did to the bees. I *know* you went out of your guidelines, so tell us what you did."

I straighten, and my desire to laugh in the face of danger dissipates. My nerves thicken into rage at her accusation. "I didn't *do* anything to them."

"Are you sure about that?" Brooke snarls.

"Yes, I am! Would you lay off for a minute? Not everything that happens is my fault." I shout, my blood boiling.

Everyone is staring at me, surprised by my abrupt response, so I hurriedly add a soft, "Sorry...I'm sorry. It's the fever messing with me."

Brooke frowns but doesn't reply. My palms are clammy, and I force myself to slouch into a non-threatening position. It's not her fault that I'm a mess, that the experiment went wrong, that the bees are *not* bees anymore.

Norman claps his hands together, pulling us back into reality. He points at Brooke and I. "You two need to work together to find a solution."

I open my mouth to protest, but he beats me to it.

"That is a *very* firm order." He clicks his tongue. "As for the rest of you, I suggest you all make yourselves busy with other tasks around the Nectar. She needs a deep clean." He turns to walk out of the room but pauses. "Try not to let me catch you fucking in the halls."

Norman departs quickly.

I flex my fingers, trying to work the frustration from my body, but it lingers like a disease. There's no way I can work with Brooke on a solution. Fear creeps in as I stare at the floor. How am I going to figure out what's wrong with the bees now?

"We should get moving," Brooke says as she passes me.

I follow after her like an obedient dog.

"Jensen," Connelly calls out to me, but I hold up a hand to silence him.

He's the *last* thing I need to be thinking about right now.

# 23

I lean against the cool steel wall as I sit on my bunk, flipping through my grandfather's notebook that I stole from the backpack June found. I trace the languid curves of his handwriting. He took copious amounts of notes on Galactica while he was here, and like me, he was attracted to the Hive. It was here before him too. Naturally, he was entranced and spent his time studying the structure, curious about how it came to be, but he never found the answer.

A pit hollows in my stomach as I turn the final pages of his journal. There are no words on them, only images, poor simple sketches made by my grandfather. His depictions turn my stomach—carefully drawn bees evolve into monsters with each page turned. On the final page is the creature I saw in the Hive, a human-sized bee accompanied by the words: *I will be one of them soon. I didn't mean to. I am sorry.*

The echo of footsteps captures my attention, and I shove the notebook under my pillow. June walks into the bunkroom. Her arms flex as she climbs the ladder to her own bunk. Her black hair is braided back over her shoulders. She pauses midway up her ladder, turning toward me. An ache pulses within me at the sight of her, and I swallow.

"You're staring," she says.

"Oh, yes, um." I can't help the blush that rises to my cheeks. I try to remind myself it's only the infection drawing me to her.

"We need to tell the crew what we found," June says. She stares down the tunnel that leads to the rest of the quarters of the Nectar. "They should know about the creature."

A burning sensation floods me. Under no circumstance can the rest of the crew find out about the creature.

"Why?"

"It might help us understand the infection." She climbs back down her ladder. "Maybe the people who came before us got infected too. Maybe they have an outpost with supplies we could use."

"I don't think that would be helpful," I say. "The creature has nothing to do with the infection."

"*Humans* were here before," she interrupts me. "And they're *not* here now. What do you think that means? Hmm?" She raises both brows. "If your grandfather didn't kill them then that creature is the only other explanation!"

I shake my head, stammering.

"That *thing* out there could be the reason they never returned." She laughs, wildly. "Admit it."

"There could be thousands of reasons they didn't come back," I say, averting my gaze. "We can't say for sure that they ran into the creature. Besides, we were infected through *my* bees. How does that have anything to do with the creature?"

"Did you stop and think that perhaps the creature infected your bees?" June asked. "It's a large ass monster-pollinator. You think that it wouldn't consider interacting with the bees?"

I hadn't thought of that, but even so, I have to stifle a nervous laugh, my face heating. "Scientificially—"

"Shut the fuck up about the science for a minute and *think* about it!" June glares at me for a long moment. "Either way, you know they're dead, and soon we will be too."

I bite my tongue and search her devastated face. She's angry and scared. Sweat drops occupy her forehead, and her cheeks are flushed. But she's wrong. She *has* to be wrong.

"They'll kill it, June," I say, small and weakly, sniffling. "They won't let me study it. You know Connelly will go out there and kill it."

*He will kill it, and I'll never know if it is my grandfather or not.*

Her lip trembles, but she says nothing. Telling them about the creature is a risk because in turn, I will have to reveal what the creature did to her.

*Because it's the right thing to do.*

"Okay," I say, running a hand through my curls. "Let's tell Norman."

"Thank you," she says, a single tear trailing down her cheek.

"What creature?" Connelly leans in the doorway, a cigarette dangling from his mouth as usual. He looks between us, brows furrowed.

"Well?"

June turns to Connelly, but before she can get a word out, she falls, hitting the ground hard. I fly out of my bunk and Connelly rushes to get to her. Her body seizes a few times before stilling.

"June? June?" I ask. "Are you okay?"

She takes a shaky breath. "Yes. Sorry." She sits up, touching her forehead. "I'm a little warm. Must be all this talk about the infection. It's getting to me. Perhaps I should go to the med bay and see Keller. Can you come with me?"

"Dr. Keller is already there," Connelly says. "She's plenty fine to help."

We help her to her feet, and she takes off without a second glance. My stomach curls in tight knots. June's getting worse, and *fast*. Great concern floods my mind. She's the only one of us who has been touched by the creature, but if she's right about the bees being manipulated by it, we could all be facing the same fate. Distracted as I am, I don't even notice when Connelly moves to his bunk, settling down and lighting another cigarette.

He doesn't even try to talk to me. Tension fills the space between us, it's unnatural. He's been nothing but kind to me, even giving me the space I asked for. Maybe Brooke is *wrong*.

I approach his bunk cautiously, positioning myself against the metal ladder and look down at him. "Hey, we need to talk."

"Do we?" He readjusts his pillow, still not giving me his full attention.

"I'm sorry..." I shuffle my feet. "For the lab and how I acted. I think I got too in my head with everything going on."

He tilts his head to meet my gaze and offers me a small smile. "Don't worry about it, Jensen. We all get stressed." He crosses his legs and leans forward and pats an empty spot on his bed. "Sit. I hate it when you hover."

I do as he asks, clasping my hands in my lap. He pulls off his green jacket, leaving him in a black muscle tank. He holds up a pack of cigarettes, offering me one. I shake my head and he tucks them under his pillow. His eyes narrow as they meet mine, the smoke from his cigarette obscuring his face slightly.

"Tell me about the creature."

With no other choice, I say, "It lives in the Hive."

"The Hive?"

"I went back and June came with me," I explain. "We found a few things…human belongings."

He puts out his cigarette against the wall, sitting up. "Human belongings?"

"Yes…" I hug myself, rubbing my arms. "Remnants of my grandfather's crew."

Embarrassment grabs me by the throat, dragging me under a sea of rising panic. I cannot stop the torrential downpour of fear warping through my body. We, like my grandfather, will die here if I don't tell Connelly everything.

I choke on all the evidence; my grandfather's sketches, his apology, the humanity in both creatures' eyes. I hiccup, a sob ripping from me. "June and I were attacked."

"By this creature," Connelly prompts.

I dig my nails into my arms as I echo out the truth. "By my grandfather's creature."

His brows furrow. "What?"

"The bear-creature… the one from the Hive…" I laugh with tears streaming down my face, my body shaking. "My grandfather made them—morphed the poison from the bees into something large enough to be used as a weapon, and I think these weapons attacked his crew."

"But The Company said—"

"I *know* what The Company reported," I snap. "But that's not what happened."

"You can't be certain," he challenges. "You say you found this creature in the Hive, but it doesn't mean it has anything to do with your grandfather."

"Of course it does! I have his journal, his plans, his *plot!*"

My screaming echoes around the room. All at once, I feel every ounce of anger and grief ripple out of me. I'm drained, near to collapse. Connelly and I stare blankly at each other as my nervous system clicks offline completely.

"Okay," Connelly says, soft and understanding.

Goosebumps scatter up my arms. We both know what must happen now, but I'm not ready to face it. I'm not ready to hate Connelly for it either. I'm not *ready* to let go. Numbness envelopes me like thick fog.

*I need to feel something.*

"Will you kill it?"

His expression softens. "I'm sorry."

The sting of his words penetrate down to my gut. He's a liar. I know he's not sorry.

"No, you're not."

Connelly lets out a shaky breath and lightly touches my thigh. The way his thumb draws circles on my leg almost sparks something in me, but nausea overtakes everything—erasing the flames that usually grow in his presence.

"What can I do to make this easier for you?" he asks.

I rest my hand over his, stopping his movement. He's warm, gentle, safe. I should be grateful that he's willing to risk his life to protect all of us—to protect *me*. But, I'm not.

"You can't make it easier." I grind my teeth together. "I have to move through this alone."

"No, you don't." He tilts my chin up, the sensation of his callused hands against my face is grounding. "Let me hold the weight of this wound for you."

"It's not yours to carry," I whisper.

"I don't care," he whispers back. "Let me carry it anyway."

He leans forward and brushes a tender kiss against my lips, but I feel nothing. I push him away, shaking my head. He grabs my hand and pulls me roughly into a hug. It's there that everything falls apart—*I* fall apart, and he's there to catch the pieces.

# 24

Connelly's already cracked open a bottle of bourbon before the rest of the crew arrives at the mess hall. He pours two glasses neat and slides one across the table to me. I palm it before taking a small sip. It's smoky. Better than the one we had before landing on Galactica. He sits next to me, pressing his shoulder into mine.

I hate that I've cracked wide open for him. And even though he's met me beautifully with each moment of my vulnerability, I despise how much he knows me deep down. I never should have let anyone get so close.

One by one the rest of the crew trickle into the mess. June and Norman carry two platters of food from the Nectar and place them in the center of the table. Tomms trails in last with a pile of plates and silverware. Dinner's a nice serving of corned beef and potatoes. We're all at ease now, warm food and liquor in our bellies. Connelly finishes first and pushes his plate out of the way.

"I have a proposition for you, Captain," Connelly says, leaning forward.

Norman cocks his head to the side. "I'm hoping you're not bringing yet another problem to my attention."

"Well..." Connelly chuckles. "Yeah, I am, *but* I have a solution."

"Go on."

"Dr. Jensen has brought it to my attention that there's a bee-like alien living in the Hive that's violent in nature," Connelly explains. "She and June discovered it."

My attention turns to June, who, by all means, looks better now than when she nearly fainted. She seems distant as if she's not in her body.

"Another alien?" Brooke asks, voice high-pitched.

Norman tosses his fork onto his plate, the clattering noise scrapes my ears. "And the solution?"

"I'm going to go kill it." There's no happiness in Connelly's tone. He points to Tomms and June. "I'd like to take my best shots with me too. Just in case."

"Hell yeah," Tomms says, reaching across the table to slap Connelly's hand.

Norman's face isn't lit with delight, but he nods along. "You're okay with this death, Dr. Jensen?"

I can barely get myself to speak, but I know what I need to say. "Why wouldn't I be?"

"Connelly said it's a bee," Norman says flatly. "I thought you might care to weigh in on the decision."

"It's fine," I say.

"I agree with Captain Norman," Brooke says. "I find it hard to believe that you wouldn't want to study the creature. It's a *bee* Hannah."

I can't meet her eyes. "Death is a part of the circle of life."

She snorts.

"Lay off," Connelly barks out. "Jensen says it's fine, so it's fine."

And it *is* fine with me, this death, because it satisfies Connelly. However, this doesn't seem to be the case for June who is visibly upset. Her shoulders slump as she hangs her head and quietly excuses herself from the table.

I'm not the only one who notices. Norman does too. I jerk my head in her direction, and he follows her. The rest of the table continues discussing Connelly's expert plan to kill the bee-creature, and I draw out a map to find its lair.

# 25

Research notes are splayed across the table. Brooke flips through one of my folders on honey bee biology from graduate school. I try to keep my focus on the pages in front of me and not spy on her. I don't want her to run across anything too private, but I'm sure she's scanning the margins anyway, remembering I used to journal in them.

I skim the one I'm reading, trying to come up with a hypothesis that would explain the mutation that's *not* the creature. But we're not dealing with honey bees at all which makes it hard considering my knowledge is almost exclusively about them. Still, their sudden change in biology and their ability to transfer behaviors onto humans is unheard of.

*Which means it's likely the creature's fault.*

I pray the contagion's origin will not turn us into similar dark monsters.

"If you keep your thoughts to yourself, they will swallow you whole, *and* we won't make any progress toward a solution," Brooke says. "I can see the furrow of your brow intensifying. Please, if you do have a hypothesis, share with the class."

I gulp. "I don't believe the honey bees *are* honey bees. That's all I've got."

She raises a brow, still focused on the document in front of her—a new folder with my notes on Galactica.

"Did the bees not seem larger to you? More lengthy in shape?" I pose, hoping to distract her from thinking about my grandfather. "You said it yourself that their behavior was predatory."

"Could be a mutation of the natural environment." Brooke shrugs, setting down the folder. "Invasive species can sometimes adapt strangely to their environment."

"Yes but the mutation was rapid," I counter. "They need ten days minimum to mature enough to mate. Besides, there's not a queen in each hive. Not since I had to replace them."

"Have you considered haploid selection?"

"Are you trying to suggest a *reversal* of haploid selection?"

"The environment could have an effect on the specimen storage," she says.

"That still doesn't explain the rapid reproduction rate," I argue.

Brooke shrugs.

"Sometimes—" she says casually as she picks up a brown leather journal, flipping through the pages. "Sometimes other causes are the source of such change."

*Other causes? What is she implying?*

"A pity that such an original source isn't catalogued in The Company's library." She cracks the spine of the journal and opens it to the very first page with a grin on her face as she reads, "Journal of Rick Carlson. October 12th, 2146,"

A pit forms in my stomach as I recognize the journal in her hand. All the dots start connecting. I know that journal like the back of my hand, memorized every faded line of the sketches of mutated bees and my grandfather's scrawled handwriting in the margins. I don't need Brooke to read it. I know exactly what it says.

*Needle bees.* My grandfather's magnum opus. The reason for his downfall and the reason I came to Galactica.

They were meant to be used for quickly administering life saving medication. It's no wonder why my bees looked so familiar. The longer stingers could deliver higher volumes of medication within the first two layers of human skin. It's what they were theoretically programmed to do, so what if the behavioral properties of the mutated needle bees were being transferred to us?

The pit in my stomach grows into a chasm. Every fear and worry falls into the darkest parts of my being.

"You know, I've been wondering about your research proposal for this mission," Brooke says. Her lips twist, and she flips to the next page in the journal. "It was a fascinating piece of literature."

"Thank you," I say stiffly. *Why is she bringing this up?*

"I heard you were nominated for an award."

"I was—am," I correct.

She chuckles. "An epic discovery. Ground-breaking scientific research. It might change the future for all of mankind."

I clamp my mouth shut.

"I wonder how much of it was stolen," she says, her voice laced with the same accusatory venom as when she discovered the truth about our thesis project. She waves the journal in my face. "You never did learn your lesson did you?"

"It's not a crime to be inspired. "It's a weak defense, but there's not much else to say. We're at a crossroads.

"Oh, Hannah, plagiarism doesn't win awards." She sets down the journal. "Real scientists can actually form a hypothesis *and* conduct an experiment. You have never been anything more than a fraud."

I stand abruptly, my chair falling over behind me. "Will you stop?" I screech. "We're not twenty-two anymore. I *have* my degree, and I earned it. This mission was *my* idea!"

She looks at me skeptically. "No? You didn't steal this one from your grandfather?"

"I didn't!" I want to slap her, to rip her hair out, to peel her skin from her face. "That's why you're here isn't it? To spy on me and ensure that my research is *actually* my own? To make sure I didn't fuck this one up like he did?"

She reels back, confusion and accusation flickering across her face. "What?" She shakes her head, scoffing and crossing her arms over her chest. "What? Are you serious? No. No, Hannah. That's not..." Her nose scrunches up in that all too familiar way. "*I'm* not here to spy on you. I might hate you, but I wouldn't lie to you. I'm *better* than that."

I swallow, and even though I don't want to know, I ask anyway. "Who?"

"Who else?" Brooke sneers. "You want to know what Connelly really does back home?"

*No.*

"He's a private investigator."

I nod, unable to help the rush of tears forming. I knew the mission offer was too good to be true. The Company is clever. Brooke was planted to distract me while Connelly did the real work.

I twist my shirt in my hands. "Do you know what will happen to me once we go home?"

"I imagine it depends on what Connelly discovers," Brooke says sharply, disgust curling her lips. "The Company doesn't tolerate liars or frauds. If they found out this entire mission was developed by Dr. Carlson, I imagine they will float you."

She glances at the papers strewn across the table. All of

the evidence collected and created over years. If Connelly needed proof that I cheated my way in life, he'd have it. He only needed to scoop up my grandfather's work and compare it to mine. He would know I'm not only here for the bees. I'm here for answers. I should destroy it, my grandfather would say the same, but my heart won't let me. It's all I have left of him.

Brooke clears her throat.

As if reading my mind, she confirms my worst fears with no trace of empathy on her face. "He's been through these already, so no need to throw them away."

I open my mouth to tell her that he didn't take anything, but she must have anticipated that because she cuts me off.

"He made copies."

# 26

Connelly is spying on me. My lungs grow small as I stumble through the hallway of the Nectar. I can hardly believe that The Company would go to such lengths to bring me down, but it makes complete sense. No wonder he knew so much about me prior to the mission. I can't believe how *flattered* I felt thinking he *cared* about me.

I stifle a sniffle, wiping my nose as I pause in the middle of a corridor.

*How could he do this?*

Buzzing thrums somewhere deep in my mind— my vision fades in and out. Faint wings beat nearby and I search for the intruder. Saliva coats my tongue. Distraction takes root within me. Somewhere on this ship I am being called.

It comes to me in a sharp vision. Tongue against cheek. Water washing over freckled skin. An image of me in the field surrounded by bees that he conjures in order to get hard enough to stroke himself.

*Am I in Connelly's head?*

The vision—I can't fight it, and I can't fight the ignition of fire within me. My heart swells, and my breath hitches. His image of me is beautiful.

*God, what I would do to taste her. She must be so delicious.*

I dart out my tongue, unable to help myself as desire spreads through every fiber of my being. He wants me as badly as I want him. I clench my thighs, an insatiable need takes control of me.

*I pump my hand faster, chasing the high of my ecstasy as I envision her kneeling before me. Her mouth wraps tightly around my cock, so beautiful, such a good girl...*

I turn sharply and press my forehead against the freezing metal wall of the Nectar. I breathe in synchronized breaths, counting down from one hundred in threes.

"Get it together," I tell myself.

Steam embraces me, the humidity nearly suffocating. I hear his voice, a soft, *"Jensen..."*

Now he's in *my* mind, infiltrating my every thought, brushing his fingers against the inner workings of my mind, down my cheek, across my neck...

*"Please..." He begs. "I need you."*

Beads of pleasure filter through me, and my back arches. The Nectar's wall feels good against my breasts. I don't pay attention to anything but the sensation of my nipples chafing the inside of my shirt, the coolness of the metal, the growing throb between my legs. I slip my hand into my pants, brushing my fingers lightly against my clit. It's like a drug—like ecstasy to touch myself. A breathy moan escapes me.

I hear footsteps, but I don't register his presence until his chest is pressed against me.

*"There you are."*

I crane my head back, resting it on his shoulder as he slips his hand in to join mine. I know I shouldn't trust him. He's been lying to me, but I don't resist as he slides a finger against my wetness, swirling it around until I'm locked into a daze.

"How did you get to be so beautiful?" he whispers.

His breath tickles my ear. I shudder.

*My strokes grow faster, impatient. I can hardly breathe at the sight of her. Curling desire builds and builds, and I'm almost there.*

My heart pounds to match his pace. I can't help but press my ass into him. His hard length brings another whimper from me.

"Shh." He chuckles. "You'll get what you want. Be patient."

*I can't.*

A burning sensation climbs within me. I attempt to move my waist to the stroke of his fingers, speeding us up. He pins me flat against the wall with only room for his hand. I let out a cry as stars of pleasure burst over me. This is so right, us together. Damn the consequences if he is spying on me. I have a need only *he* can fill.

Dr. Keller and Dr. Jensen are to report to the mess hall immediately.

Connelly's hand disappears and I am brought to the present. I'm alone, naked in the corridor, pressed against the wall of the ship. The Nectar repeats the order. A tingling sensation sweeps up the back of my neck and across my face. I quickly dress myself and curl my arms around myself as I rush toward the mess hall.

# 27

"I'm pulling the mission," Norman says firmly, slamming his bourbon down on the table. His watery bloodshot eyes are all the evidence needed to know that he's piss drunk

We're alone in the mess hall, but there's six plates set out. The others are coming which means Brooke and I have only minutes to convince Norman to stay before more voices of reason enter the room. I give a sidelong glance at Brooke, and she gives me a curt nod.

"We discovered what's happening," I say, coming up with the most realistic lie I can, "if you give us a few days we can create a vaccine. We only need time to run the calculations."

"No," Norman says.

"Why not?"

Norman chuckles, taking a swig of his drink before shouting at the ship again. "Tell them what you told me, Nectar."

Navigation Officer Mari June attacked Chief Military Commander Arthur Connelly at 14:23.

"Don't be short on them, honey," Norman chuckles. "Injuries?"

Injuries were sustained.

"Where are they?" I ask.

Norman only shakes his head. "You're missing the point, sweetheart."

"Oh, you *are* drunk," Brooke says as she rounds the table, snatching the bourbon bottle and glass away from him. "You should be ashamed. We have an emergency situation on our hands and our captain decides to get wasted?"

"You would too if you realized how bad things are about to get for us." He stands and shows us the back of his hand. There's a tiny bandage on it—he's been stung.

"Oh, please. We're all stung, and we're fine," Brooke says.

I tune them out, moving toward the speaker in the wall that the Nectar's voice comes out of.

"Nectar, where is Connelly?"

Location undisclosed.

"What? Why?" I turn back toward Norman and Brooke. "Why won't she tell me?"

Location can only be disclosed to approved personnel due to Protection Clause 132.

Tears pool in my eyes. I look at Brooke; I've never been so desperate. Spy or no, I *need* to see Connelly. Norman only laughs. Brooke shakes her head and lets out an exasperated noise.

"Nectar. Override Protection Clause 132," Brooke says.

*What? Why is she helping me?* I wipe my nose, utterly shocked.

Norman drops his smile. "Don't you dare."

Personnel identification number needed.

"Brooke Keller. ID code 567AH9." Brooke places both

hands on the table and leans forward until she's leering over Norman. "You are pathetic. You need to get it together, or else—"

I don't hear the rest of Brooke's threat because the Nectar's voice floods the room.

Location: Medical Bay, Hatch Four.

I'm out of the room and racing through the halls of the Nectar before I think to ask where June is located, but she doesn't matter to me. The lights of the Nectar turn from their normal silver to a deep red; an alarm sounds from somewhere far away. Rationally, I know that Brooke and Norman have gotten into an altercation, but I can't bring myself to worry about either of them, but that doesn't matter either. All that does matter is Connelly's health and safety.

The medical bay's windows give a clear view of the hatch doors. Everything is in place, even the cryo-pods at the other end of the room. I punch in my identification number and scan my fingerprint. As soon as the door unlocks, I'm flying across the empty room, but the sight of blood stops me in my tracks.

Dark red spots turn into large smeared handprints leading to Hatch One. The window peering into the hatch is foggy. Is that where June is?

*Connelly.*

I whip my head toward Hatch Four, and it's clean, untouched. He's safe.

I swallow. I *need* to know where the blood is coming from. I take a step toward the hatch. It's made of titanium, with three padlocks, and a window on top reinforced with wire—safeguards for patients in the event of intruders. They're designed to be impossible to break into, but to break out of? The lights above me flicker. Soft groans sound from behind the door. I shouldn't check. Whatever is behind Hatch One isn't meant for me to see. Another cry propels me forward.

"June…?" I whisper.

If she's behind that door she can't hear me. I take a breath and try to rationalize that no one in their right mind would put June, who *attacked* Connelly, three doors down when we have a cell for imprisonment. Norman wouldn't do that.

Unless he thought she was ill. *Okay, that might be rational.* Trembling, I creep even closer. The door is only a foot away now. I could reach out and touch it if I wanted…The locks aren't fully sealed. My stomach churns.

A bloody hand slams against the window, and I stumble backward, but before I can lose my nerve, I regain my footing and lunge forward and secure the locks. Whatever is behind the door, June or not, is not getting out.

"What are you doing?"

I scream, my heart thundering away as I turn toward the voice. Connelly is leaning against the frame of Hatch Four, smoking a cigarette as if everything is right as rain. My hand flies to my chest as relief fills me.

"Oh, it's you…" I laugh, wiping away a stray tear from my cheek. I hadn't realized I'd been crying until now. "You're okay."

His brows furrow, and he gestures to Hatch One. "What were you doing?"

"Oh, I—" I freeze as my attention lands back on Hatch One's door. It's open and there's no blood to be seen. The floor is spot-clean. Even more worrisome, there's no one inside Hatch One. The lights are off and the bed is made.

"What?" I *saw* blood. Someone was in there making noise, moaning in pain. But… I can't deny what's in front of me. *I need my meds.* But when I reach into my pocket, they're not there. My bottle is missing. *Shit.*

"Seeing things, are we?" he asks, chuckling.

I spin around. "It's not funny. I heard a girl—June. I saw a bloody hand."

"Your mind is getting away from you, Jensen." He shrugs. "I'm the only one here."

"I thought…" I take several deep breaths, rolling my shoulders back. "It doesn't matter." I cross the space between us. "What happened?"

Connelly tugs up the sleeve of his green jacket to reveal a large bandage covering half his forearm. Slowly, he peels it back and reveals a bite mark. The bite is clearly human-made, the skin around the punctured and raised. Yellow ooze seeps from the edges of the wound. It's infected. "Doesn't hurt." He sucks in a breath through his teeth as he retapes the bandage and covers his arm. "Much."

"June *bit* you?"

"She didn't mean to," he says, letting out a puff of smoke. It billows out in an O. "It's the infection."

I can't wrap my mind around it; why would June bite him? The sting's venom can't be the cause of this violence. No one else is experiencing these symptoms, but will we start to? We can't go on like this. For a split second I conjure up the image of the bee-creature in the Hive. Is that our fate?

"Why the long face?" Connelly reaches out to rub my shoulder. "What's going on in that pretty mind of yours?"

"I…"

I pull my attention away from Connelly's bandaged arm. I'm unsure why I hesitate to confide in him. His worry seems genuine, but he's too relaxed. I take a step back, breaking his grasp on me. A frown mars his face.

The med bay door opens behind me, and Brooke stands in the threshold, breathless and sweaty.

"Brooke? What's wrong?"

Her gaze flickers between me and Connelly.

"June's missing."

# 28

The bars of the cell are bent inward. June's natural strength wouldn't have been enough for her to escape in this way, but she was gone and nothing else could have done it. I stifle nervous laughter as we gather around the evidence. I still can't wrap my head around the idea that a rabid superhuman June has vanished.

June is morphing into a bee creature, I am sure of it.

We need to leave this planet *now*. Before something worse happens.

Connelly's back is to me, and I swallow as another consideration comes to mind. June's bite might be as infectious as the bee's sting, which means that Connelly could inherit her newly developed traits. I have to fight back the rising panic. If Connelly became rabid too... we would *have* to leave him behind. I *can't* leave him here. Even though he could be my end, I can't stomach the thought of losing him completely.

"What's the determination?" Norman asks.

The captain leans against the far wall, more sober now thanks to Brooke's intervention. He's missing his uniform jacket, but the rest of his clothing is ironed out. Brooke must have forced him into a shower and new clothes. A good call since he reeked before.

Connelly kneels next to the cell and pulls out a pair of black latex gloves, slipping one on. He brushes his finger against one of the bars and when he tugs it away, yellow slime follows his finger. I clap my hand over my nose and mouth, Brooke follows suit..

"Everyone should mask up," Brooke says, her voice muffled.

Tomms snorts, and Norman approaches Connelly.

"Well? What is it?" Norman asks.

"I'm unfamiliar," Connelly says. His pupils dilate, entranced by the material. "Does anyone else recognize it?"

Only Brooke is brave enough to take a step forward even if it is a hesitant one. The substance is sticky; when Connelly pulls it apart, it stretches like taffy. We all wait with bated breath for anyone to reply, but no one knows what it is. Norman lets out a groan and runs his hand down his face.

"Shit," he curses.

"Shit is right, Cap'n," Tomms says, clapping his hand on Norman's shoulder. "You're *finally* getting the hang of it."

Norman only glares at Tomms which is enough to get him to back off.

"I think we can follow it," Connelly says.

We turn our attention back to him. He points to the ship's floor. A path left by the substance and June's sticky footprints leads down the hall. How we didn't see it before, I don't know. Must have been in too much of a rush to see the evidence of June's disappearance for ourselves.

Connelly gets up and nearly sprints down the halls of the Nectar. All four of us were hot on his heels. In the chase, the halls seem smaller than they are. The pipes and wires lining the ceiling, and the steel walls box us in. Connelly bypasses every exit until we get to the airlock. He stops in his tracks, and I nearly collide into him.

It's not because the airlock was open that Connelly stopped. That wasn't unusual since the air is so similar to what we're used to, it's what was on the other side of the airlock that brought him to a halt.

A pool of blood rests in the center of the airlock's chamber and on top are patches of skin. *June's skin.*

"She's not dead," Connelly states, "but she could be soon if we don't find her."

"That's a lot of blood, man," Tomms whispers.

"Not enough to bleed her out." Brooke bends down and uses a pen to poke at the skin clumps. "It's strange…almost like she's shedding."

"Molting," I correct, absentmindedly.

Brooke nods her agreement. I shuffle past Connelly to join her, but I don't crouch low. The stench is enough to ward me off from further curiosity. Beyond Brooke are the sealed doors that lead outside. There's a bloody handprint near the seal, not unlike the one I imagined on Hatch One's door. She's lucid enough to use her identification number to get out.

"She's left the Nectar," I say.

"Where would she go?" Norman asks.

There's no telling where she'd go. Nowhere is safe, and beyond the Nectar there is no shelter from nature. A thought nags at me, telling me that's not necessarily true. The bees found shelter, didn't they?

"The Hive." A nervous chuckle bubbles from my lips. "She's going to the Hive."

"What? Why would she do that?" Norman asks.

"It'll be her first instinct," I say. "There is no doubt in my mind that if she is transforming into one of those creatures—

and I am sure she is— she'll go to the only place she knows none of us will dare trek."

The cocking of a gun pulls my attention. Connelly arms himself to the teeth with the weapons from the side panel. Tomms follows suit. Even Brooke stands. They're going after June, and I have to go with them. I pat my side, ensuring my pistol is still holstered to me before grabbing another gun. There is no telling how much June's condition might have progressed in the few short hours she's been gone.

"You can't all go out there," Norman says. "It's not safe."

"Stay behind then," Connelly says. He opens the outer door and spares me only a glance before stepping onto the ramp that leads to the beach. "I'll take Tomms and Jensen with me."

I give a nod of thanks to him and walk out into the warm air. Brooke lingers in the threshold of the door. She reaches up, typing in her identification number.

"We'll be right here waiting for your return," she says.

The outer door seals shut, and we're left on our own.

"I'm gonna need you to tell me everything you know about the Hive," Connelly says as we approach the Hive's lowest entry point, the same one we used before. "Weaknesses. Strengths. All of it."

I try not to let my annoyance show, but I'm sure it comes across in my tone as I reply. "Well, I'd know more if you ever let me actually study it."

"Anything at all might help."

"It's a *hive*, Connelly," I say. "A structure meant to be a home for a colony of bees. That's it."

Connelly peers at me over his shoulder. "Yeah, and what did you learn on your little extra expedition?"

I frown. "I already told you—a creature, like the bear, but insect-like. Presumably it'll have unknown characteristics, but mostly, it's fast."

He gives a curt nod and proceeds forth into the Hive. I follow close behind, and Tomms brings up the rear. We creep up the all too familiar staircase into the structure. Molten walls of orange and yellow encase us.

Connelly pauses as we hit the first intersection, holding up a fist. I brace myself, scanning the area in front of us. I don't see what he sees. I want to ask why we've paused.

Then I hear it—what he's hearing. Quiet screams of pain. The noise is blocked by something. Connelly takes another moment to listen before he proceeds at a brisker pace. We're not yet jogging, but we're moving with purpose. My old military training takes over and I keep my wits about me. We clear the lower levels quickly with Connelly as lead then make our way to a large chamber in the center of the Hive.

I try not to let my shock overcome me. The room is like the one Connelly and I initially discovered, but there are thousands of egg-shaped sacs covering the ceiling, walls, and floor. And right in the middle of it is June.

Tomms steps forward, gun still drawn. "June!"

She doesn't turn around at the sound of her name but she begins to twitch. At first it's slight but gradually it becomes more noticeable until she's practically seizing. Without thought, I bolt toward her, but Connelly grabs me. He doesn't have the spare arms to wrestle Tomms into submission.

"Tomms!" Connelly whisper-shouts after him.

Tomms is halfway across the room when June abruptly stands. She spins to face us, and horror fills me. Two dark holes linger where June's eyes should be, and her skin is rotted away in patches, replaced by a yellow fuzz. She steps—no *flies*—toward us, hovering over the eggs.

Her attention is latched onto Tomms who still approaches without caution.

"He needs to back off," I whisper. My back is pressed against his chest, and he doesn't seem like he's going to release me anytime soon. I clear my throat. "You can let go of me."

"No…" he whispers. His breath is hot on my ear. "No, I don't think I'm going to…"

Annoyance flickers through me, but my focus is pulled back to June and Tomms. They're nearly touching.

"We need to get him away from her," I say as June's mouth opens, revealing sharpened teeth. Low growls trickle out of her, and she cocks her head to the side, drinking in Tomms like he's a meal. It reminds me of the bear creature from the field. She's hunting him. A spike of fear pierces me, and my insides become liquid "Like *now.*"

"I know. Stay here." Connelly lets go of me, shoving me to the side. "Tomms. Get *back.*"

Tomms tries to, but June lunges. At the same time Connelly lets off a round, and I am paralyzed with both fascination and fear. June tears into Tomms, his guttural screams echo around the chamber. Connelly moves forward with steady force, laying into June until her body slumps over. But she keeps getting up.

Heat envelopes all of us as the eggs around the room start to burst. My vision wavers, and red dots blind me. The screaming won't stop. I'm vaguely aware that they're coming from Tomms and June—but something else is too—my pulse. Sweat drips down my forehead. We're being baked alive as each egg hatches. Buzzing fills the room.

Tomms stops screaming, but June remains hovering over

him, feasting. Connelly is relentless. I know I should back him up with my own firepower, but I sling my gun over my shoulder and grab the back of Connelly's jacket, pulling him toward me instead. He stops firing long enough to look at me.

"Connelly! It's no use. We have to go." I grab his forearm and tug with all my might, but the horror on his face tells me he's not moving. "Come on."

"I'm not leaving him," he says.

"He's dead. We have to go *now*."

His face pales, but he lets me lead him out of the Hive. We run as fast as we can. Honey-slick walls slow our escape as we have to stop and pull out boots from missteps. My senses heighten, and I keep checking over my shoulder. June doesn't pursue us, but it's not until my feet hit the pollen lake that I take a breath of relief.

Connelly and I stumble into each other, and I let him hold me close as we slowly walk backwards, away from the Hive. A feral scream rings out and the Hive shakes. I can't help the whimper that escapes me as I watch the structure crack open at the top. Perhaps I was wrong. It's not a hive at all, but an egg.

"Connelly," I whisper.

"Shh…" He clamps a hand over my mouth.

Swarms of bees break from the Hive and with them are two bees that are larger than all the rest. They're both human-shaped. My knees wobble, and Connelly has to hold me up, dragging me backwards with him.

I want to scream or cry or curse at myself. This is my fault. I should have *never* brought us here.

# 29

The full ramifications of what's happened don't hit me until we're safely back in the Nectar where I promptly slip into pure dissociative shock. June's symptoms increased rapidly over a twenty-four hour period. She was fine yesterday, and today, she's as good as dead. She's dead, and she killed Tomms, and *all of it is my fault.*

Brooke sets a glass of water in front of me, and I can barely get it down with my meds. I listen quietly as Connelly relays everything to Norman and Brooke. Neither of them can believe it, the loss of two crew members on a mission that shouldn't have been dangerous at all. Even Norman tears up for a brief second, but he snaps back to command mode once Connelly finishes.

"Nectar!" Norman shouts. "Prepare launch sequence."

Error. Cannot compute launch sequence.

"What error?"

Hydraulic leak in corridor two.

"Hydraulic leak?" Connelly's nose wrinkles.

Norman sucks on his teeth. "Override error alert, Nectar. We're launching."

```
I am afraid I cannot override without
authorization.
```

"I'm authorizing you," he says. "Jasper Norman. ID Number H2CA561."

```
Authorization denied. Company override
needed. I cannot damage Company property.
```

My pulse races. Norman beats his fists against the table.

"Damn you, Nectar!" he shouts.

"Can we fix it?" Connelly asks. He leans his head back and shouts at the ship. "Can we fix it?"

```
Affirmative.
```

"I'll do it," Norman says. "I'm the only one left who knows anyway."

I let out a long breath, knitting my hands together. But my relief is short-lived. I can't return home now that my mission has killed two crew members. The Company will surely see this as a means to remove me from academia, and Connelly will have concrete evidence against me..

*I can't return with witnesses.*

So, what? I kill everyone and return by myself? No, that won't work. There's a good chance Norman knows nothing about The Company's investigation, and Brooke has turned a new leaf. Killing Connelly isn't an option because—*because I don't want to. But he's a spy. He'll ruin me.* Brooke would never agree to it...maybe if there was a scientific reason to leave him behind and—*can I really do that to Connelly?*

I take a few steadying breaths before saying, "We can't go back." I stand and grip my gun. "Not all of us."

I aim at his chest, and my bottom lip trembles. He's saved me more times than I can count. He's been good to me, and he sees me, the *real* me, but I can't let him come back with us. He will ruin all of it.

"Jensen?" Connelly asks, voice cracking with question.

Brooke arms herself, pointing her gun not at Connelly but at me.

"What are you doing, Hannah?" Brooke asks.

I gesture toward Connelly with the tip of my gun. "Allowing him to come back with us would violate quarantine protocol."

"What?" Brooke asks.

"June *bit* him. He's infected," I say, my hands shake.

"We're *all* infected," Connelly bites back. He takes a few steps away from me, his hand reaching toward his gun as he finally understands I'm serious. "By that logic we should all stay behind."

I shake my head. "It's different. June was stung by the creature before we were all stung by my bees."

"Everyone, lower your weapons, please," Norman urges. "I'm sure we can talk this out in a more civil manner."

My gaze seeks out Brooke. I need her to trust me on this because it's true. Given the timeline of June's transformation, I'm certain she was infected by the creature that attacked us during our trip to the Hive. Hers was different and more aggressive than the rest of ours—we didn't mutate. It's the only explanation that makes sense. I urge Brooke to read my mind even though I know she can't. She lowers her weapon.

"She's right," Brooke admits.

"Are you sure?" Norman asks.

Brooke nods. "You saw what happened to June. Do you really want to travel back to The Company with another creature on the loose?"

Norman's attention shifts to Connelly, only a small trace of pity lingers within them. "I'll leave you all our leftover supplies."

"What?" Connelly laughs. "You can't be fucking serious." He turns to me, but I can't face the betrayal in his eyes. "Hannah?"

"The Company will send a rescue team," Norman says, flatly. "I'll ensure they do myself."

My stomach drops, and I grow dizzy. Connelly's expression filters through several emotions before he storms out of the room. The rescue team will take years to return here, and by the time they do, Connelly will be long dead. I'll be free. Horror creeps over me, consuming me alive bit by bit as I realize I've handed Connelly a death sentence out of pure selfishness.

*How could I do this?*

Waves of shame crash over me, and I turn away from Norman and Brooke so they can't see my face fall. I breathe through my teeth, blinking away my tears. I'm just as horrible as my grandfather was. I murdered two, now almost three, of my crew members all because I wanted to know what happened to my grandfather.

Norman tells us to be ready for launch in two hours. In the meantime Brooke and I are to haul all of our extra supplies onto the beach for Connelly to survive off. Every step shatters me, knowing I'm leaving him behind, but I have to do this.

It's not an insignificant amount of supplies either. He has camping gear for six, food for years, seeds to plant, all of the tools he could ever need, Norman had us leave him weapons. I'm certain I would have been left with less.

We finish unloading all of the supplies, and I'm soaked through with sweat. What I want more than anything is a long shower, but I won't be comfortable taking it until we're far from Galactica's reach. I lean against the Nectar, watching the sun in the distance. Clouds of orange drift over her, covering even the brightest of rays.

Footsteps clang on the ramp, and Brooke appears, freshly dressed. I'm jealous she feels safe enough to clean up. But then again, she didn't see what I saw in the Hive. She has no idea what's happening to us at all, what Connelly will become in a few short days.

"Norman says it's t-minus thirty. We should board," she says.

I give her a thumbs up. That's all I can manage. She leans over the side of the ramp until she's level with me.

"That was a bold move back there," she says. I don't have to ask what she's referencing. I grimace. "What would you have done if I didn't agree?"

"Killed all of you," I say a little too seriously so I throw in a laugh.

Thankfully, she laughs back. The tension dissipates between us, and I ease up my stance. Brooke's the most unlikely of allies between us, but she *is* an ally, for now. After silence falls over us once more, I catch Connelly's figure wading out into the pollen lake.

"I should let him know we're leaving." I kick off the Nectar, propelling myself forward. Before I'm able to move out of her reach, she grabs me and I'm forced to turn back.

Her face softens. "Hey, I'm sorry."

My confusion must show because she continues without prompting.

Her lips turn up slightly. "I know you and Connelly are close. This must be extremely difficult for you to let him go, but you're making the right decision. He would ruin you."

"I don't have much of a choice." Not if I want to continue pursuing my career when we get home.

"There's always a choice." Her gaze locks onto something behind me. "But...you...made...the...right...choice..."

Her voice fades into the distance as I slowly turn on my heel. My nails dig into my thigh through my pants. Dots pop up in my vision, and my heart starts to race. A smoky scent infiltrates my nostrils and I look over my shoulder. In the distance, the Hive is burning.

*No, no, no, no, no.*

"What is this?" I rip myself out of her grasp. "A distraction?"

"Hannah—"

I'm already racing toward the Hive. My feet hit the pollen lake, and I'm consumed with terror as I watch the structure burn. A fire starts within me, burning every single fragment of my being. My heart is ripped in two. The sanctuary that calls to me is crumbling. Brooke catches up to me, tackling me into the water. She holds me as I scream and scream and scream.

It doesn't take long to collapse in on itself, then there's nothing left at all. Tears stream down my face as pure grief takes hold. I'm not sure why I'm crying so much. I was never going to see the beauty of the Hive again, but I'm devastated. Every trace of proof that I didn't do this to our crew was in that hive, every clue to exonerating my grandfather too.

"Why am I so upset?" I gasp out between sobs.

"It's the venom." Brooke pets down my hair, she's crying too. "The infection. That's all."

I wipe the tears from my face, allowing myself to be held in her arms.

"Let's get back to the Nectar."

Out from the fire treads Connelly, his face stained with

ash and soot. Rage unlike any other takes hold of me. They orchestrated this together. I stand up, turning on Brooke. I'll kill them—both of them, now. They deserve to die for what they've done to me. But before I can say anything, the Nectar explodes.

# 30

Light. Fire. Wind. Pressure. Ringing. Laughter. All of it fills the air.

We're stranded on Galactica and I am laughing a full-bellied laugh. Until blood fills my mouth from where I bit my cheek, and I stumble back, coughing it up. The taste of iron floods my senses, and I can't get a breath down. A hand pats my back. Connelly is there, saying something to me.

I reach into my pocket to find it empty. My medications were on the ship. I'm helpless now. For some reason, that makes me laugh harder through the tears.

Slowly, it gets easier to breathe, and I can face the sudden death before us.

No one says anything as we trudge back toward the wreckage and scrap through it. There's no return home. Brooke and I are trapped with Connelly who will inevitably transform into a killer bee and murder us.

We're stuck. We're defeated. We're dead.

I hear Brooke's wail over all the buzzing. She exhausts herself crying. I'm tempted to join her, but I wait, utterly numb.

Silently, we finish setting up Connelly's camp. Nobody wants to talk about our bleak outlook on survival. Connelly might have burned down the Hive, but we've all been stung. Our desire for one another will win out, and there's no telling what Connelly might do. He could bite us, and one by one we will turn alien like June. We are destined to destroy one another. It's only a matter of time.

Connelly wastes no time busting out the liquor. I want to tell him it's a waste. We're numb enough already. Who needs any further distraction?

"Should we make a toast?" he asks, raising his glass above his head. "To the death of Nectar, our last chance of going home?"

Brooke pours herself a glass, and I follow suit. Her red-rimmed eyes meet mine. Her face is puffy with grief. We all raise our glasses before downing our drinks. It burns my throat, burying itself deep in my chest with the rest of my secrets and lies and horrible truths.

I was always going to fall one way or another, like my grandfather did. We were all doomed, except maybe Brooke, who might have had a chance at a good life.

Both Brooke and Connelly pour another round, but I set mine aside. Guilt crawls over me, and all I have are the flickering flames to distract myself.

"They were some of the kindest people I've ever known," Brooke says, her voice scratchy. "June especially. Always so attentive to everyone and nice. Too nice."

"She was," I whisper, but it feels disingenuous coming from my lips. The only time she'd done something nice it resulted in her getting injured, infected, and now, she's dead.

Connelly doesn't try to add to the conversation, he only downs another glass and lights a cigarette. Brooke keeps going, with tears leaking down her cheeks.

"Norman was brave, and he cared about us. Even when he was bossing everyone around, he did so like a protective brother," she says. "I really looked up to him."

My stomach coils in knots and the heat of the fire warms my cheeks.

"Tomms—"

"I'm glad you loved them," Connelly interrupts Brooke. "Really, and I'm sorry they're dead. I didn't know anyone very well but Tomms. He was a *pain* in my ass, but he was an okay guy." He pauses, pulling out his pack of cigarettes and tossing it between his hands. "I'd have more cigarettes if it weren't for him though, so for that alone he's a bastard."

Brooke's lips twist. "Seriously?"

Connelly's mouth falls open, and he shrugs. "Listen, it's going to be a long few days."

"Who cares about your cigarettes?" she says, her voice pitching up.

"Well obviously me," he laughs.

Brooke stands, throwing down her glass. It hits the sand and rolls away from us. She's fuming.

"Are you fucking kidding me?" She's practically yelling now. "I get that we are stranded, but at least we're alive! Can you be a little more sensitive?"

He holds up his hands like he's getting arrested.

"And you!" She points at me. "Don't think I haven't already put two and two together."

"What?" I blink hard several times because I have no idea what she's implying.

"You blew up the ship." Brooke's hands ball into fists and drop to her side. "You stole our chance at survival because you're that selfish, and really, you always have been. I should have seen it sooner."

*What?* Pure shock hits me like a brick, and my mouth hangs open.

"I didn't blow up the ship," I say, looking wildly between them. "I swear."

"No one else had motive!" Brooke shouts.

"I think it was an accident," Connelly says. "It's no one's fault. It just happened."

Brooke glares at him. "I know you don't believe that. You've seen how she is."

It takes a moment for him to respond, and my heart hammers as I wait to hear what he has to say. Will he take her side? Will he accuse me?

He doesn't. He simply stares Brooke down and says "I do, actually."

"*What?*" Brooke is seething.

"I *believe* her," he states, lifting his chin.

"Whatever," Brooke says. She turns her heel and begins to storm off but stops at the edge of our camp. She looks over her shoulder at me, the anger in her eyes is unnerving. "I know you did this, Hannah."

I pull my gaze away as she walks away. I dig my nails into the palms of my hand. Iron floods my mouth, and I wince as I continue to dig my molars into my cheek. I must calm down. I slowly count to ten in my head, trying to relax each muscle group in my body as I go. We can't turn against one another now.

"I didn't do this," I whisper. My voice is shaky. "But I know you don't trust me. There's no point in lying."

Connelly raises his brows. "What are you talking about?"

I level my gaze with his, trying to be open and honest. "You know my grandfather came here before us, and a part of me *is* here to prove that he didn't kill his crew. I've read dozens of his journals and studies. I thought there was no way he snapped all of a sudden. The mission was too important to him."

Connelly sets his drink down.

"But...he did. I'm almost certain the creature in the Hive was him." I take a deep breath, and keep going. "He killed his crew with his experiments, and without meaning to, I brought all of you here to die."

"You're being too hard on yourself," he says, his voice soft and gentle. "None of this is your fault, even if you wanted to come out here to discover the truth."

"The truth?" I ask, laughing even with tears streaming down my face. "Isn't that what you're after?"

He shakes his head, tilting it to the side.

"You have been spying on me this whole time," I say, gesturing to Brooke walked away. "She told me that you took all of my files and made copies."

"What?" he says incredulously. "I...Why would I—"

"Just stop." Tears prick at my eyes. I am so utterly alone. I have *no one* who cares about me. "It's fine, Connelly. I knew before we even..." I hiccup. "Whatever, it's fine."

"Hannah—"

"Stop." I hold up a hand, silencing him. "I know you're investigating me for The Company. There's no point in lying about it because we're never going home now."

Connelly lets out a long exhale. "How could you believe that?"

"How could I not?" I ask, my voice cracking.

He stands and walks away. I nearly fall apart but Connelly returns from the dark with a tub in his hands. He slams it down on the beach, sand spewing out from the sides as he tosses the lid away.

"I wasn't copying your research to spy on you," he says,

his voice shaking with anger. "I made copies of all of your research because I knew someone was after you. I wanted you to have your things should shit hit the fan. *Which it has.*" He gestures around us. "I don't know how you could think for one single *second* that I would do anything to harm you."

My chest tightens. I'm at a loss for words. In the tote are dozens of binders, vials, and journals. He took not only copies but originals. There are even copies of the binder Brooke and I were using for the cure. All of my research, all of my *grandfather's* research... all of it is here.

"Connelly..." I shake my head, not wanting to believe what's in front of me.

He circles around the tote to kneel in the sand before me. He takes both my hands in his own, his eyes shining.

"Hannah, I would *never* do anything to hurt you," he says, again. "Don't you understand how I feel about you?"

I shake my head, unable to stop the choking noise I make. He cups my cheek, holding my gaze on him.

"Even if you blew up the ship, even if you destroyed our chances at survival, I would still love you," he whispers. "I love you and that beautiful, insane mind of yours."

"But you have to know that I *didn't* kill Norman," I choke out. "I don't want to die here."

I break down in his arms, every ounce of grief hitting me at once. I didn't strand us here. Connelly wasn't spying on me. Everything is a lie, and everything is ruined.

"I know," he whispers in my ear as he brushes my hair with his fingers. "I don't want to die here either, but maybe we don't have to."

"No one is coming to save us," I protest, wiping the snot from under my nose.

"Maybe not right away, but mission protocol has a drone check in after six months past our return date."

"We will be long dead by then." I sniffle.

Connelly gestures toward the tote. "Not if you continue working on your cure."

There inside the tote of Connelly's devotion is the solution to our problem. His love for me might be our salvation.

# 31

I slam awake at the sound of my tent zipper opening. Before I can even jolt up, a warm hand slaps over my mouth and I'm pushed back onto my sleeping bag. Brooke hovers over me. Even in the dark the pure terror on her face is visible as she lifts her finger to her lips.

I can barely catch my breath as I whisper. "What's going on?"

"I found something," she says, searching my face. "Hannah, I found something awful."

"What is it?"

Brooke quickly glances over her shoulder. "It's about Connelly."

I try not to let an aggravated sigh slip out of me. Already, I'm irritated. I don't want to listen to another word she has to say about Connelly. "Go on."

"I went back to the wreckage, and I found one of the black boxes. I thought maybe I could prove you were back at the ship and messed with the wiring or hacked the Nectar. I knew if I could find the recording I could prove it," Brooke says, rushing through her story. "But I found something much worse. An argument between Norman and Connelly that went south. He... Connelly, he—" She chokes up. "He..."

I grab both of her arms, shaking her and demanding her focus. "Brooke. What did you find? What did he do?"

"He blew up the ship," she says, her voice cracking.

*No.* I let go of her, scooting as far away as I can. *No, he wouldn't do that. He has no reason to do this, and he has every reason to help me get back to The Company.*

Brooke presses forward, wild-eyed. "He *killed* everyone here, Hannah. Do you understand me?"

My initial instinct is not to believe her because Connelly proved to me that he cared. He was so angry that I accused him of spying. He couldn't have possibly done this, could he? Unless he lied to me. Maybe he saw a coincidence and decided to cash in on my vulnerability.

"Why would he do that?"

Brooke said Connelly was here to investigate me, to bring me down once we returned. It wouldn't make sense to trap us on this planet unless... Unless he didn't want to complete the job anymore. But, he could have said he found nothing. Why strand us on Galactica? Why doom us to death?

"Don't believe me?" Brooke asks, snidely. She holds up a tiny black recorder. "Fine."

The recording plays, and Norman and Connelly's voices drift from the device.

*"Captain, don't make me do something I don't want to do. Please, hear me out."*

*"Not now."*

A pause, then, *"Her research could change the world if she just had a little more time."*

"I'll spare you the rest," Brooke says, turning it off. "The rest is too...upsetting."

My hand flies to my chest, and I shake my head, unsure what to say in the wake of the recording. Without thought, I launch myself out of the tent, knocking Brooke over in the process and barely making time to grab my gun. Dawn is starting to creep over the horizon. The camp is settled, and the fire from the night before is nothing more than simmering coals. I head toward Connelly's tent and hear Brooke scrambling out of mine.

Footsteps sound behind us. I turn, aiming the gun at Connelly as he approaches. A cool breeze sweeps over my legs, so exposed in my pajama shorts.

Connelly stops in his tracks, eyeing the gun as he slowly lifts his hands in surrender.

"What's with the gun?" he asks, his mouth twitching up on one side.

"You tell me," I say, unable to hide the nervousness in my voice. "What did you do to the Nectar?"

A frown flickers briefly on his lips. "I...What are you asking me?"

"Did you blow up the ship?" The pollen lake's sand is cold between my toes as I take a hesitant step forward. I focus on the tiny grains, relishing in the grounding sensation it gives me. "Did you kill Norman?"

"The explosion killed him," he replies, lowering his hands.

"An explosion you set!" Brooke breaks out from behind me. She presses against my side, hovering over me like a wasp.

Connelly clenches his jaw, but his glare is reserved for Brooke. "Norman would have brought the infection back. He didn't care about the preservation of the human race."

"And you do?" I ask.

His lips part and a soft sigh escapes him. "You care about

the infection, and I care about you. What more do you want from me?"

"Don't listen to his bullshit lies," Brooke warns. "He will kill us as soon as he gets the chance."

"That's rich," he replies, chuckling. "Didn't you say that about Jensen last night?"

She did...So why the switch up? And why didn't she let me hear all of the recording from the black box? *No, she said it was too upsetting. She's only trying to protect me.* But still, her change in attitude unnerves me.

My finger shakes as I place it on the trigger. Through the sights, my gaze locks onto Connelly. A faint red dot hits his forehead. All I have to do is pull the trigger and he'll be dead. I shift slightly on my feet, enough to give me a better look at him. He's not concerned, that much I can tell. He lifts his chin, exposing his neck.

"Think this through, Jensen," Connelly says. "Who has had a vendetta against you the entire time? Who kept putting my name in your head? Who is *really* the enemy here?"

"Just shoot him already," Brooke says. Her voice is tense and high-pitched.

But what Connelly said gives me pause. He's right, after all. He's not the one who drew suspicion to himself. Brooke did. She's the one who kept pushing me to suspect him, she's the one pushing me to kill him now.

I study Connelly closely. He's staring down Brooke with a challenge in his eye, and Brooke stares back—bottom lip quivering.

"Hannah," Brooke says again, an edge to her voice. *"Shoot him."*

Brooke might be scared, but it's not of Connelly. It's something he knows.

"I saved everything you needed to make a cure," Connelly

continues, refocusing on me. "I'm the one who protected you."

Brooke chuckles. "You blew up our only chance to go home. You delivered us a death sentence."

*But he didn't.* Not truly. Not if I can make a cure.

"You only care about saving yourself," Brooke says. "You knew we were going to leave you here to rot."

I would have. But...

*No.* I blink hard, trying to clear my mind. A dark buzz starts to envelope me, pushing every coherent thought I have down into the pits of my stomach. Either of them could be lying to save themselves.

I square my shoulders, tightening my stance. "Who are you protecting me from?"

He takes a step back.

"Oh, come on! You can't possibly believe him," Brooke says. "You don't know him, Hannah, not really. You *know* me."

It hits me then—I *do* know her. She's been after me for years and this was her opportunity. She wanted me to suspect Connelly so I wouldn't notice what she was doing.

"You're right." I shuffle my feet. "I know that you've hated me since our college days."

"Why would I do anything to ruin your career knowing it reflects on me?"

I shake my head. Brooke knew what happened to my bees too quickly. Almost as if she'd been reading from my grandfather's journal. And why would she know Connelly made copies of my things? Unless he caught her doing the same.

"How did you know about the needle bees?" I ask. I swallow hard.

"I read it—"

"How did you *really* know that's what happened? How

did you know The Company swapped them?" She doesn't need to answer. It's plain in the twisting expression on her face. She's been caught. I could laugh at the drop of her jaw. "You swapped them. You wanted me to fail."

*What else has she been lying about?*

"Hannah…" Brooke reaches for me, but I turn on her.

"What *else* did you do to my bees?" I shout. Swapping them wouldn't be enough, she had to have done something else. Something to make them grow quicker. It hits me clearly, the only thing she could have done. She used her serum.

My breaths quicken as I line up my shot. Brooke doesn't get a chance to look surprised before I pull the trigger. I stare at her lifeless body laying in the sand.

Connelly approaches slowly and stops by my side. "That's cold, Jensen."

"Did she really try to frame me?" I ask, my attention still fixed on Brooke's idle form..

He wraps an arm around my waist. "I believe she was trying her best to."

I nod, numbness filling my body as the ringing echo of the shot whistles in my ear.

"This isn't your fault," he says in a comforting tone.

"Maybe it's not, maybe it is," I say. All the energy drains from me, I don't want to talk about it anymore. I'm tired of the anxious games we've been playing. I just want to enjoy what might be one of my last nights alive.

I rotate, grabbing his hand and leading him back to my tent. "I don't want to talk at all, is that okay?"

"Oh?"

He follows me inside, and it takes only seconds for us to settle onto my sleeping bag.

"Are you okay?"

I shake my head, and without thinking, I run my hand up his thigh, resting below his cock—silently asking permission. He raises a brow, and I cock my head to the side and blink. I want him to distract me.

He leans into me, brushing his lips against mine as he whispers, "Don't tell me then, let me help you forget the horrors of this world."

Connelly buries his hands into my hair, tugging my head back so he can trail kisses along my throat. I let out a breathy gasp, already soaked through for him. He traces his free hand up and down my spine. In one swift movement, he grabs my waist and plants me in his lap, pressed against his hard length. I can't help but grind against it.

"Good girl," he whispers, licking his lips as he pulls my shirt over my head.

He takes his time with my breasts, tugging and teasing and licking until I'm nearly undone. The pressure is almost unbearable, and my body demands release. I don't know why I'm enjoying it so much. I just killed someone, but this is pure senselessness and I want to give in.

Connelly slips a hand into my shorts, brushing his fingers against my wet center. He lets out a soft moan. I rise to my knees and take my shorts off. I want him *now*.

"Eager?" he chuckles.

He flips me over. I arch my back, my belly pressed against the soft blankets. He rests his palm against me.

"Fuck, you are soaked."

He teases me with his tip, dragging it up and down my slit. I squirm, trying to back onto him, but he pins me in place. He thrusts into me and I can't help the near scream that erupts from me. My core tightens, and I am sent into pure bliss. Connelly holds himself fully in me, waiting.

"Please," I beg. I need him to create fiction.

Like a feral creature, he unleashes himself on me. He pumps in and out, and I moan loudly. He grabs the back of my neck, bending over me and bites deep into my shoulder. The pain and pleasure is overwhelming. He keeps me close to the edge, but slows as I start to fall. Over and over again he teases me until he grabs a fistful of my hair and yanks me up so my back is against his chest. He brushes his fingers against my clit before rubbing them in a rough circle. His breath is hot in my ear.

"You're mine to protect, forever," he says. "Do you understand?"

I can barely breathe, but I manage a choked, "Yes."

He pushes me back down, slamming into me harder this time. Everything tightens into a coil, then burning heat descends upon me. My orgasm crests, and I can't help but bury my face into my pillow as I let out a sharp cry. Wave after wave of stars capture me. When it's over, I can barely remember my own name.

We lay there for a while, breathless in my tent under the Galactican stars. Buzzing lingers in the back of my mind. Saving us is completely up to me now. It's my job to keep us alive until rescue comes—*if* rescue comes. I glance at Connelly as he begins to snore.

I can save him, if I work quickly enough. Now there is nothing stopping me from discovering the truth—not that it ever really mattered. There was never going to be any truth true enough to erase the horrors that haunt me. I'll never be forgiven or seen as a hero for bringing us here knowing the risks. Maybe that's alright. *Maybe* that's my punishment.

THE END

# Acknowledgments

I'm going to keep this one short and sweet. So, big thank you to all the bug girls that picked up this book (and everyone else who was either forced to read it or thought it was going to be an intense sci-fi and was pleasantly surprised). Thank you, reader.

Thank you to Maggie because this book nearly broke us, but it was so much fun to splice it all together. Quite literally this book wouldn't have released without your hard work. I'm forever in your debt, and I feel so lucky I can voice memo you my insane ideas.

Thank you to my early readers: Meg, Nikki, Jinapher, and Max. You all are the best critters around.

Lastly, thank you to my family, my pets, and Steel — I love you all.

# About the Author

Rowan Redfield is an adult fantasy and sci-fi author. Rowan is known for Reveries — the multiverse that all of their books take place in. In their free time you can find them playing TTRPGs, puzzling, or spending time with their fur babies.